HANNAH'S STO

The Men of Space Station One #10

Marla Monroe

MENAGE EVERLASTING

Siren Publishing, Inc.
www.SirenPublishing.com

A SIREN PUBLISHING BOOK
IMPRINT: Ménage Everlasting

HANNAH'S STOLEN MEN
Copyright © 2014 by Marla Monroe

ISBN: 978-1-62741-665-8

First Printing: August 2014

Cover design by Les Byerley
All art and logo copyright © 2014 by Siren Publishing, Inc.

Printed in the U.S.A.

PUBLISHER
Siren Publishing, Inc.
www.SirenPublishing.com

HANNAH'S STOLEN MEN

The Men of Space Station One #10

MARLA MONROE
Copyright © 2014

Chapter One

Hannah peered up at the two men staring down at her. She wasn't sure what they were going to do now that they knew they'd been tricked. Fear tightened her throat to the point that she could barely draw a breath in, much less let it out. Her lungs burned with the effort.

"What the hell do you mean she sent you instead?" the one named Edward asked in a deceptively quiet voice.

"S–she changed her m–mind about going. She m–made me come in her place. She sent this for you." Hannah pulled the envelope from her pack. Edward snatched it from her hand.

She looked up at the other man standing in front of her. His handsome features remained unchanged as if he hadn't just been told that the woman he'd married had skipped out on him. His stoic silence scared her even more than Edward's obvious anger.

"Why?" he finally asked, when Edward turned and stalked off a few feet to read the letter.

"She had a boyfriend and didn't want to leave him. He wasn't eligible because he had a record." Hannah looked down at her tightly clasped hands, trying to make them relax to no avail.

"No. Why did you come instead? Why didn't you just say no?" he asked.

She knew his name was Porter. He was large like a porterhouse steak, but without the fat. He had broad shoulders and a chest as big as a mountain. His weather chiseled face looked as if it had been carved from stone. If it wasn't for his amazing green eyes and all that thick wavy brown hair, she'd have thought he was statue come to life. The hair and piercing eyes gave him just a breath of humanity though, giving her hope that he wouldn't strangle her for her part in the mess.

"When they started rounding up all the women who didn't have Shear's Disease to go underground, my younger sister tested positive for the disease even though she was only twelve. They were taking me, but they wouldn't take her even though it would have left her all alone. Our parents had died a month before in a fire from the first wave of riots. We had no family close by. I couldn't leave her by herself," she said, praying he would understand.

"What does that have to do with why you're here?" he asked.

"I paid Gladys's brother to forge her health papers, so I could take her with me. It took them a few days to get to us after we had our physicals. Her brother hacked into the computer and changed the test result to read negative and gave us copies."

"And Gladys threatened to have your sister retested by telling them what you'd done if you didn't take her place," Porter finished for her.

"Yes. I'm sorry. I didn't know what to do. It was all so fast. All I got to do was pack the one bag and say good-bye to my sister." Tears spilled from Hannah's eyes despite her resolve not to cry. Men hated tears.

"How old is your sister now? Hell, for that matter, how old are you?" Edward demanded.

"I–I'm twenty-five. Cathy is sixteen now. I had another sister who would have been nineteen, but she was killed in the fire, too." Hannah didn't know why she'd added that last part. Maybe because she felt like Jeni should matter, too, despite being gone.

"What is going to happen to your sister with you gone?" Porter asked, walking back toward them as he shoved the folded envelope into his pocket.

She swallowed. "We made friends with a few other women there who will watch out for her with me gone. I–I was hoping she might get chosen to come here one day, but if they test her again before they marry her to someone, well, she wouldn't get to go and they might kick her out of the bunkers. I guess I'll never know what happened to her now."

"Hell, Porter. It's getting late. We need to grab our things and go. They warned us not to travel at night." Edward picked up her bag along with one of his and strode in the direction of the transport that had been assigned to them.

Porter grabbed one of the large cases in their pile and followed the other man. Hannah didn't know what to do, so she picked up one of the heavy cases and struggled to carry it to where they were loading the vehicle. Porter looked up and saw her walking in their direction with the case in her arms and cursed before nearly running to meet her.

"Don't pick anything else up. You'll hurt yourself. We'll handle the loading and unloading. You just wait till we finish and we'll get you strapped in." He carried the case she'd nearly broken her back hauling as if it were a feather and not a ton of bricks.

Where they going to let her stay with them? Did they really have much of a choice? She was all they had. She couldn't stop the icy cold finger of fear from digging through her gut at the thought of living with them. She knew nothing about them or what to expect of life with them.

Oh, she knew about the planet, they'd been well schooled on how to survive on Alpha, from planting and harvesting a garden to the dangers that surrounded them there. She even knew a little about what to expect their sex life to be like, but she didn't know anything about the men themselves. Were they normally kind men or were they grumpy? Did they enjoy talking or would they expect her to stay quiet?

Ever since the sun had begun to die, sending larger and larger amounts of radiation toward Earth, people had been trying to figure out what to do. They'd already started traveling to other places to set up colonies as part of space exploration, but now that their sun was in the act of slowly imploding, they had to speed up the process and find galaxies with their own healthier sun to explore. Three planets had finally been located that were considered habitable to humans. She had ended up on a craft destined for planet Alpha.

In the years leading up to the initial colonization, they found out that a large majority of the woman on Earth were now sterile due to Shear's Disease, which occurred in women between the ages of eight and forty-five. They had discovered that the increasing flares and explosions from the sun as it slowly winked out of existence was directly linked to the female's inability to become pregnant. There was no way to avoid it other than to hide the women below ground in specially made bunkers designed to withstand the constantly increasing radiation and magnetic fields produced by the sun.

The two men loaded the last of the trunks and cases then turned to where she still stood waiting, having been afraid to move from the spot Porter had left her. They shook their heads and exchanged glances. Porter walked over and took her elbow in his massive hand.

"Let's get you settled. We've got to stop by the storehouse to get some perishables. Everything else has already been set up for us. We just have to show up," he said as he picked her up so that she could climb into the buggy. "Remember never to climb in or out of one of these things if the engine is on. It's dangerous."

"I know. They instructed us while we were on the trip here. I just spent six months on that thing just like you and they crammed a lifetime of lessons into such a short amount of time," she said.

"I hope you were a good student," Edward grumbled. "This isn't going to be a bed of roses. There aren't many luxuries here, and you can't pop into town to shop whenever you want to."

"Edward," Porter said in a warning tone.

The other man didn't say anything else, but by the set of his jaw, he wanted to. Hannah wondered what she'd landed in this time. After Gladys found out they were in the same area of the bunker, she'd used the knowledge she had about her sister to get anything she wanted from Hannah. She'd more than paid for what she'd done to keep her sister near her. Now it looked like she was in for even more karma.

"What's your name?" Porter asked her as he strapped himself in next to her.

"Hannah Engels."

"Well, Hannah. I'm Porter Jones and that is Edward Stafford. This didn't turn out like we planned, but we'll get through it. Just do what we tell you to until we get things unloaded tonight and we'll have a long talk about the situation later. Okay?"

Hannah nodded her head. "Okay. I'll stay out of your way."

Edward grunted again then started the transport and pulled away from the loading dock. It occurred to her that they were officially married to Gladys who was back on Earth and she was going to be living with them without being married at all. Considering this wasn't Earth and there wasn't really anything she could do about it, Hannah supposed it was the least of her problems.

The fact that she had two men to please was something for her to worry about. Why did they have to decide on two men? She knew the reasoning behind it, but it didn't help settle her nerves about it. They'd looked at the conditions on the new planets and likened them to when settlers had first arrived in America. The conditions were harsh and the land dangerous. They'd decided that considering there were so few women who could bear children, it was only logical to pair them up with two men. That way they had more men on the planet settling it and working the land without the fights that often broke out over the lack of available women.

On the other hand, the women had two men to take care of her so that if one was away working, the other could be close by to keep her safe. That had been a problem with the original settlers of the West on Earth. When the men had gone to tend to the cattle or take them to market, the women were left vulnerable to attack. With two men, one should always be nearby to defend her. She couldn't help but wonder how that was working for the settlers who'd been on Alpha for a while now. She'd heard there were children now.

She'd been on board with a female doctor who'd come to be with her husbands, one of which was Space Station One's only doctor and the other his nurse. Megan had told her all sorts of things about how since the first settlers had arrived more than twelve children had been born and all were healthy. The settlement itself was nearly six years old now. The first year and a half there had only been the men working to build the town and initial homes. They'd started a ranch and several farms that produced their major grains, hay, and corn. Once they had everything ready, the first women had been sent to choose their husbands.

Hannah nearly laughed out loud at Megan's rendition of how that had gone over. It was decided after that to pair the families up before the trip over and cut down on the time it took to court and win their wife. Plus, they'd taken to using computer programs to match the two men with a compatible female. Where did that leave her and the men?

"What is that?" Edward's voice cut into her thoughts and she looked where he was pointing off in the general direction they were traveling.

"Fuck! I think it's one of those mantis things. They're supposed to be extremely dangerous and aggressive," Porter warned.

"What the hell do we do? Wait for it to go away or just keep heading toward it and hope it moves?"

"It's going to be dark soon. I don't want to still be sitting here when it happens. Veer to the right of it as much as possible with these trees, and let's see what it does," Porter suggested.

Hannah gripped the straps of the harness holding her in the seat in a death grip as Edward started aiming for the wooded area on the right. They all kept their eyes on the oddly shaped creature that seemed to be watching them as it remained seated where it was. The closer they got, the more detail she could make out about its shape. It resembled a cross between a praying mantis and some sort of big cat. It actually had some fur and paws. It didn't look to be more than about four feet, but she'd read they could stand on two legs which would make it much taller.

"That is one ugly son of a bitch," Edward said. "It has to weigh nearly three hundred pounds. Look at the size of it!"

"Keep us out of the trees, man, and I'll let you know if it heads this direction."

"Well, give me some warning because they can move fast, according to the literature," Edward told him.

"So far it's just watching us. We're going to be even with it in a few more minutes. Hold steady." Porter didn't take his eyes off of the animal.

Hannah was afraid to watch the tree line since Edward was skimming by them pretty darn close. The mantis seemed the lesser of the two evils at that point. It wasn't nearly taking their doors off—yet.

"It's turned its body toward us, Edward, but it isn't moving. I think there's something behind it. Maybe it's guarding its food or something." Porter had one hand on the dash trying to see around Edward's profile now that they were about even with it.

"I think it has a baby with it. I saw it move, Porter," she whispered loudly.

Edward chuckled. "Why are you whispering, Hannah? Afraid it can hear you?"

She glared at him, uncaring if he saw her or not. He was being an asshole. Sure she had taken the place of the woman he'd married and now he was stuck with her, but she hadn't had much of a choice either.

"Crap. I can't see it anymore now that we're past it. You're going to have to keep an eye on the screen from the cameras. I think Hannah is right though. I think it was trying to make sure we didn't see its baby or come after it." Porter shook his head. "That was one ugly fucker."

"Hope there aren't any waiting around on us when we get to the house. I don't particularly like the idea of unloading this thing in the dark as it is," Edward said.

"It's going to be dark when we get there?" she asked.

"Yeah. Not full dark, but close. At least there are two moons here. That will help with visibility to some extent, but not enough to suit me." Edward kept looking at the monitors that showed the view of what was behind them. So far there was no sign of the mantis or anything else for that matter.

"When we get there, stay right there until one of us comes and gets you to take you inside. Then stay inside. Got it?" Porter asked her.

"I've got it." She didn't like being treated like a child. She hadn't been a child in a very long time. Taking care of her sister and the way things had changed so fast back on Earth had aged her far more than her mere twenty-five years.

"Keep an eye out for any more of those things. I don't want any surprises if we can help it," Edward told them.

Hannah scanned ahead of them while Porter watched out the side window. It was starting to grow darker as they raced toward their new home. When Edward started slowing down, she jerked her head around to stare at him. As if sensing her worry, he looked over at her.

"We're here. Our new home should be right over that little hill."

She held her breath, waiting for them to reach the top to get her first glimpse of her new life. When they got there, Edward drew to a halt so that they could all gaze down at the two-story house set slightly away from the trees that surrounded most of the land their house was built on. It looked to be a nice-sized house. They'd been told there were four bedrooms. It was expected that they would start having children right from the start. It had been part of the contract everyone had to sign. Of course, Hannah hadn't signed the contract, Gladys had.

"So what do you think?" Porter asked.

"It's pretty," she said.

"Looks like our closest neighbors are about a mile away. See that roof outline over there?" Edward asked.

She nodded. She wondered what they would be like and if they had children yet. She wondered what her two men would be like to her and if they were going to be happy with her or wish they'd never been a part of the colony. Then a horrible thought occurred to her. What if they decided they didn't want her at all and told her to leave? Where would she go? Was there somewhere in town she could stay? Would they even let her?

Hannah's entire trip had been wrought with worry that someone would discover her secret and she would be sent back to Earth. Now that she was here, an entirely new set of worries kicked in. What if Edward and Porter didn't want to have anything to do with her once they got to know her? What would they do with her? The thought of being alone on a strange planet where no one wanted her scared her to death. Panic hit hard, leaving her teary eyed as she looked out at her future, one she now had no control over if she ever had in the first place. The two men sitting on either side of her held it in their hands. With Porter, she felt like she might have a chance to win him into giving her a chance, but Edward didn't seem to like her much. Suddenly the idea of returning to Earth didn't sound like a bad idea anymore.

"Let's get going, Edward. We need to get this thing unpacked before full dark," Porter said.

"Think you can handle unpacking while we unload?" Edward asked her with a frown.

"I'm not an idiot or a child. I'll unpack," she said, staring at him.

"Just wondering what you know about how life is going to be here. I don't want to have to constantly be watching you to be sure you don't end up in trouble," he said, obvious displeasure on his face.

"Edward. What the hell is wrong with you?" Porter asked.

"It's okay, Porter," she said. Turning to Edward, she smiled. "I attended every class on the ship and can handle anything that has to be done. If you want to know the truth about it, you should be glad it's me and not Gladys since she's lazy and hates anything that requires her to get her hands dirty. I'm not a spoiled woman, Edward. Gladys was very spoiled and very mean. Now get moving so we can get on with our lives. I'm sure you have a lot you need to attend to before we eat tonight."

To her shame, tears spilled from her eyes, but she refused to wipe them away and draw attention to them. Instead, Hannah looked straight ahead as Edward took them down the hill to the beginning of the rest of her life.

Chapter Two

Edward felt like a total ass for the way he'd been treating Hannah. Yeah, she'd taken the place of the woman who'd been selected for them and deceived everyone, but she'd done it to protect her sister. It was obvious the woman they'd been paired with hadn't been who she'd pretended to be. He didn't know Hannah and wouldn't have believed her description about Gladys except that the woman's personality had come out in the note she'd written loud and clear. She was a very selfish person.

He fingered the envelope in his pocket before jumping down from the transport to check out the house and be sure it was safe inside. Edward dropped to the ground with a light thump as he stepped up on the porch.

"Got your gun ready?" he asked his partner.

Porter grunted and held it up.

"Let's do this then. On three." Edward counted to three before he opened the front door and let Porter aim the gun around the room before stepping inside.

He reached over to the wall and felt around till the light came on when his fingers hit the switch. They searched the entire house, making sure there was nothing waiting for them in any of the rooms. The place was nice and quite large, even for three people, but then they were expected to fill it with children as soon as possible. He sighed and followed the other man back outside.

"I'll help Hannah while you open the back," Porter said.

He nodded and watched for a second as the other man opened the passenger door to help Hannah down from the buggy. She protested when he tried to lift her down, saying she was too heavy for him, but Porter ignored her and swung her down from the transport, her hair caught his attention as it swayed down her back. He remembered the way it shined in the sun back at the station, a warm honey color with highlights of red and gold.

Why Hannah thought she would weigh too much to be picked up was lost to him. She had broad shoulders and round squeezable hips. Her breasts were slightly more than a handful and just right for a man to slip his cock between and ride them to completion. The plump, kissable lips were perfect on her cute face with her hazel eyes and pert nose. Bedding her wouldn't be a hardship by any means, but he needed to get his anger over being duped out of his system and put it behind him before they moved any further in their relationship. They had a lifetime ahead of them. Starting out on the wrong note wasn't a good idea and he'd already done that.

Shaking his head, Edward started unloading the various boxes and trunks from the transport. Before long Porter joined him and they started carting the luggage and supplies inside. When they were down to the last large trunk that would require them both to carry it, Edward pulled out the note that Gladys had sent them and handed it to Porter to read. His new friend looked at him with an unreadable expression before he opened it and began reading.

While Porter read, he kept watch around them to be sure nothing snuck up on them while they stood out in the open under the two moons that illuminated their new home. He'd nearly forgotten they weren't back on Earth while he'd been unloading the transport. Lapses like that would get them hurt or killed. He vowed to remember from then on.

"Hannah was obviously telling the truth about her being spoiled and mean spirited. I think we should count ourselves very lucky that Hannah is here with us and not Gladys. What do you think?" Porter folded the note into a small square piece of paper before tucking it inside his pocket.

"You're right, but what does that say about us?" he asked. "I mean they supposedly matched the three of us based on the questions we answered."

"She had to have lied when she filled it out. They would never have put someone like her with us. That woman needs a lot of supervision and daily spankings if you ask me," Porter said, shaking his head and picking up one end of the trunk.

Edward picked up the other end. "I'm not one for corporal punishment, but my brother might have given her a run for her money."

Porter chuckled. "I'd have liked to watch, but that's not my idea of a perfect marriage either."

Edward pushed open the door so they could walk inside the house. As soon as they made it through the door he shoved it closed with his foot and they carried the trunk through the living room to the stairs. He was happy as hell this was the last one. Carrying them up the stairs got old after the first two. Thank goodness there'd only been four with two of them his and two of them Porter's. As they dropped the heavy trunk to the floor, he remembered that Hannah had only managed to pack the one suitcase and the pack she carried like a purse. Again he felt ashamed of how he'd treated her. No woman would have willingly left for another planet without everything she could have managed to bring along.

He looked up to find her stepping out of the bathroom. Her eyes held worry as she gnawed on her lower lip with her teeth. Edward could feel the tension and nervousness surrounding her and it was all his fault. He sighed.

"Is everything okay in the kitchen?" he asked, trying to sound relaxed and less hostile.

"Um, yes. Everything seems to work fine and there looks to be plenty of food to get us started. I have soup warming and thought I'd make sandwiches to go with it when you're ready to eat," she said.

"Sounds good." Porter opened one of the trunks. "Would you mind putting away my things after dinner? Edward and I will need to contact the other farmers we'll be working with to talk over schedules and such."

"I don't mind. Do you have a preference as to how you want things arranged?" She glanced over toward Edward but quickly turned back to Porter.

"Just however you want to set us up is fine with me. Edward?" Porter looked over at him for confirmation.

"I'm fine with it, too. I'd appreciate it, Hannah," he said, giving her a slight smile.

She visibly relaxed and nodded. "I'll put everything away for you as soon as I finish cleaning the kitchen. Let me know when you're ready to eat."

"Let's go ahead and eat now, Hannah. It's been a long day for all of us. I think a good night's sleep will do us a world of good," Porter said.

Had Porter seen her stiffen when he mentioned sleeping or had he imagined it? Edward wondered if she was anxious about sharing her body with them or maybe just him. It wasn't like he hadn't given her a reason to be worried. He'd been a complete asshole from the moment she'd revealed that she was replacing Gladys. Edward figured he had a lot of groveling to do in order to smooth things over. He wasn't looking forward to it one bit.

* * * *

Hannah trudged up the stairs after cleaning the kitchen and putting away the dishes. She could hear Edward and Porter talking to the men from the other farms from the office as she passed. She knew they were living on the opposite side of the original farm where Cam, Phillip, and their wife Lacy lived. Another family lived on the opposite side. She didn't know who they were yet.

The four trunks and two suitcases were daunting to look at, but she found that once she opened them they wouldn't be all that difficult to sort out. With Porter being a little shorter than Edward, but beefier than the other man, she was able to determine which were his clothes and which were Edward's. She figured Porter was about six foot two and probably weighed close to two hundred forty pounds. He wasn't flabby by any means, with muscles and broad shoulders that reminded her of a wide mountain range. He had shocking green eyes that were mesmerizing when she looked into them.

Edward was maybe an inch taller but not as muscular as Porter. He had defined muscles but less bulky than the other man. His light brown hair was almost a dirty blond with highlights throughout that attested to his time in the sun. He had light blue eyes that seemed to pierce straight to her soul. The fact that he wasn't exactly pleased that she'd duped them only made it more difficult to look at him. She felt very uncomfortable looking into those knowing blue orbs.

Looking down at her own body, Hannah sighed. She looked like a frumpy maid around them. Gladys had definitely been more their style with her slimmer body type and long blonde hair. Where she tended to burn in the sun, Gladys tanned a golden brown, not that they'd been allowed out once they'd been sequestered beneath the earth. Still, here, she would have looked good next to them.

She shook off those thoughts and continued putting away their clothes. Both men wore boxers but Porter was more adventurous, wearing plaids and bright colors while Edward preferred primary colors. Porter wore PJ bottoms but no tops to bed while Edward wore either boxers or thermals or nothing to bed. She shivered at the thought of him wearing nothing. What would it be like to sleep with a man who slept nude?

She'd had exactly one boyfriend before they'd been pulled from their homes to reside in the bunkers below ground with only other females to interact with. The only men they ever saw were physicians and an occasional older man who checked on how things were going down there.

Jason had been a nice kid, but he'd been just that, a kid. They'd grown up together and been best of friends until it changed into something more. She wondered what happened to him. Shortly after things had gone to hell with the Earth's changes, Jason had joined a group of men who'd volunteered for the space exploration programs. He'd moved to Florida and she'd never heard from him again. Would he be somewhere on Alpha or had he been sent to another planet somewhere?

It didn't really matter. They hadn't been madly in love at any rate or he never would have left. It had stung a little at the time, but she was long over it. Now she had much more important things to worry about, namely, Edward. He obviously resented her for her part in Gladys's switch up. She couldn't really blame him, but they needed to get passed it. They were stuck with each other for the rest of their lives.

As she set up their things in the large bathroom next to one of the three sinks, Hannah realized that she'd taken the middle sink and put them on either side of her. It had seemed natural to do that. She just shrugged and made sure she had everything from the box that Porter had separated his bathroom supplies into. She broke down the box and carried it back into the bedroom. All that was left now was to put away the trunks and her suitcase.

The sound of boots on the stairs sent a feeling of panic to her chest making it difficult to draw in a full breath. This was silly. She shouldn't be nervous like this. They were going to be living together for the rest of their lives. She needed to get control of her emotions and stop feeling so vulnerable around them.

Porter stepped into the room as she started scooting one of the trunks toward her closet. He took one look at her and hurried over to take the other end of the trunk. Edward stepped next to her and reached down for the handle she held with a telling look. Hannah immediately let go and stepped back.

"There's no need for you to strain yourself with us around. Where were you taking this one?" Porter asked.

"There's a lot more room in my closet. I think we should stack them in the back and along one side," she said.

Both men frowned at her as they carried the now much lighter trunk into her closet. When they returned for another one, Porter seemed to want to say something but just shook his head. They put three of the four trunks in her closet then shoved the fourth one in the back of their closet. She'd already put away her suitcase and backpack.

"You don't have very many clothes, Hannah. Most of what you have is only good for the spring and summer. You're going to need more clothes for winter," Porter pointed out.

"I know. I figure a few pair of thermals, a coat, and a couple of long-sleeved shirts should do it. I only had warm weather clothes below ground. They kept the temperatures steady year round down there," she explained.

"You were supposed to be given an allowance to buy what you needed for the trip," Edward said.

She winced. "Um, Gladys used it to get what she wanted since it was set aside for her anyway."

"Didn't she realize you'd need the clothes? Where was she going to run off to anyway? Didn't she realize she'd end up with Shear's disease by leaving the bunkers?" Edward asked.

Hannah sighed. "She wasn't too worried about me and she didn't want children anyway. She always worried about her figure. I don't guess she cared if she developed Shear's disease or not."

"Do you have what you need otherwise until we go back to Space Station One in two weeks?" Porter asked after shooting the other man an annoyed look.

"Yes. I'll be fine. Don't worry about me."

"I didn't mean it to come out that way, Hannah. I'm sorry. I just meant that you should have had what you needed since you were taking her place. It wasn't fair of her to do that." He sounded like he meant it, but she wasn't sure if she believed that or not.

"I'm really sorry for my part in this, Edward. I didn't know what else to do. I couldn't let them throw my sister out with no one out there to watch after her. They wouldn't have let me go with her. She was all I had left in the world." Hannah's voice broke despite clamping down on the tears just below the surface. She would not cry no matter how much she missed her little sister.

"Dammit, Edward!" Porter walked over to Hannah and pulled her into his arms.

She let him hold her, but she refused to allow any more emotion to break free. She was stronger than this.

"I'm sorry. I don't know what else I can say!" Edward stomped out of the room and down the stairs.

Fear had her jerking free from Porter's hold. She didn't want him storming outside where there was so much unknown danger. Hannah rushed from the room and down the stairs to where Edward stood in front of the front door just staring at it with both hands clasped into fists.

"Edward?"

He didn't turn. "What?"

"Please don't go out there. It's too dangerous. I don't want anything to happen to you. It's all right. I'm fine and I don't blame you for being upset. This is hard on all of us. We've got to figure out how to deal with it though," she said in a rushed voice, hoping to keep him from opening the door.

The sight of his shoulders slumping hurt her even more than his storming away had. She didn't want him to feel trapped or stuck with her. She wanted him to give her a chance to make things right with him. For all she knew, he'd fallen in love with Gladys in the few short times they'd met before the scheduled launch. She had no idea what she'd said or promised them in those few meetings. One thing she did know was that she was nothing like the other woman and that might end up being the problem. She wasn't a sultry, sexy temptress who could arouse a man simply by walking into a room or opening her mouth and speaking.

Edward turned around and stared at her, his face a mask of control, but his light blue eyes seemed almost shining with emotion. She just wasn't sure what that emotion was.

"I'm the one who needs to apologize to you, Hannah. I had no right to take it all out on you. I understand why you did what you did. I would have done anything for my little sister if she'd lived. I was pissed that Gladys was able to trick me into thinking she was excited about being with us and looking forward to spending time with us. It's my pride that's stung and that isn't your fault. Please. Let's start over." Edward took a step toward her.

She wanted to believe him, but part of her still saw the shocked look on his face when he'd looked her up and down back at the station. It was obvious he hadn't liked what he'd seen. She wasn't sure how to deal with that. She'd never been able to lose weight for very long. Maybe with the type of life they were going to be leading here on Alpha she would finally get some of her excess weight off. She had a garden to plant and take care of.

She looked up at the man standing just in front of her. His expression seemed so sincere. She finally nodded and gave him a smile.

"We're good, Edward," she said.

He smiled and before she realized what he was going to do, he bent down and kissed her lightly on the lips. It was just the barest of brushes, but it took her breath, a tingly warmth bloomed where his lips had touched hers. She struggled not to lift her fingers to touch the spot.

"Let's go back upstairs. I'm ready for a shower and we all need a good night's sleep."

Hannah allowed him to steer her back toward the stairs where Porter was standing on the top step looking down at them. When he saw them heading back, he turned and disappeared down the hall. She prayed as she stepped up that this would be the beginning of a much better life between the three of them than she had expected. With her previous expectations having been so low, she figured she couldn't lose this time. At least she prayed she wouldn't.

Chapter Three

Porter stepped out of the bathroom to find Edward sitting on the side of the bed while Hannah sat on the other side. Both of them were staring in his direction as if he held the answers to all of life's questions. He'd never been in this position before. Normally he stood back and followed someone else's directions when it came to making decisions. He wasn't a leader. That was more Edward's style according to their profiles. What the hell was going on?

Instead of addressing their questioning stares, Porter finished drying his hair and tossed the towel back into the bathroom. He had pulled on a pair of pajama bottoms in deference to Hannah since he didn't know what she was used to. He preferred sleeping nude, but kept PJ bottoms at the foot of the bed in case he had to get up in the middle of the night. Of all the things they'd talked about and gone over during the six month travel time on board the shuttle, they'd never really discussed much about everyday life with their wife and how they planned to work the sex thing out.

He walked over to Hannah's side of the bed since he wasn't about to sleep next to Edward. She followed his movements with big eyes that screamed discomfort though she didn't back away as he stopped in front of her.

"Climb in, baby girl. We've got a lot to do tomorrow. I want to explore every piece of this place so I know what's out there." He didn't miss the surprise on Hannah's face. He realized it was at the fact that he'd called her baby girl. It was a habit of his to call women by nicknames. Just something he'd picked up from his dad as a teenager.

He noticed Edward was wearing a pair of boxers and slid into bed with them in place. He sighed. Looked like he better wear his bottoms for now. As soon as they were more used to each other, Porter planned to ditch his. He didn't like wearing them to sleep in.

He'd noticed that Hannah wore a large T-shirt to bed. He was sure she had on panties beneath it. This wasn't going at all the way he'd thought it would. But then he hadn't expected there to be someone he'd never met waiting for him at the station after six months of traveling across the universe either. What in the hell were they going to do?

He liked Edward. They had only met once they'd been paired together before they'd been matched with Gladys as the other third of their family triad. Though he never would have chosen to live in a triad, he'd been exposed to polyamory or poly for short. He had some good friends back on Earth who lived that way. Most of them were male friends with more than one female partner, but he'd met a few where there was more than one man in the relationship.

Edward had seemed totally on board with it from the beginning, so Porter hadn't worried that they might have to work through jealousy or resentments. Instead, he was going to have to figure out how to get them all on board with starting the relationship from scratch. He let out a breath as softly as he could. He didn't want Hannah to think he was upset, even if it were true. This just wasn't something he wanted to have to initiate.

"Hey, Porter?" Edward's voice whispered across Hannah.

"Yeah?"

"We didn't check the basement tonight. I forgot all about it until just now. Do you think it can wait until morning?" Edward asked.

"It will wait," Hannah said in a strong voice. "I don't want either of you to go down there tonight. The door is closed so nothing can get in from down there, right?"

"It'll be fine," he said. "Anything that might be down there can't get up here with the door closed. I checked and made sure it was locked, too."

Silence stretched as he tried to will his body to relax so he could go to sleep. He was used to sleeping on his right side but with Hannah in the middle, he didn't feel comfortable turning that way. After a few uncomfortable minutes, Porter gave in with a sigh and turned toward her.

"Sorry, but I can't sleep on my back," he whispered.

"That's okay. I usually sleep on my side, too," she whispered back.

"Then turn over and get comfortable," Edward's exasperated voice rumbled next to her.

She quickly turned over so that her back faced Porter and he heard Edward do the same. He'd never felt this uncomfortable in his life as he did there in that bed. They were supposed to be a family now, but having only known Hannah for a few short hours, Porter didn't feel comfortable just wrapping his arms around her and pulling back against his chest.

His cock was hard as a rock just lying next to her. She'd think he was some sort of pervert that got hard at the drop of a hat. That wasn't true at all. He could appreciate the female body like any red-blooded American male, but for the most part, he never got this hard unless he was very aroused by a woman. To his surprise and relief, Hannah did that to him. He was an ass man and she had one of the lushest tushes he'd seen in a long time. He wanted to grind his dick against it and grip her hips as he buried the shaft of his cock deep in her ass.

Thinking about it wasn't helping his aroused state one damn bit though. He reached down and adjusted his erection to a more comfortable position down the leg of his pajamas. The relief didn't last long as he tightened even more.

Porter wondered what Edward was thinking about and if he was going to make an effort at making Hannah happy or not. He liked the other man, but if he continued to treat Hannah badly, they were going to have words. He wasn't above knocking some sense into the other man either if that's what it took. Women needed to be coddled and cared for. She was going to have a tough enough life as it was without the added difficulty of living with someone being selfish and petty. No, he wouldn't stand for it. Edward was going to have to straighten up or there'd be hell to pay and he'd be dishing out the bill.

* * * *

Hannah slowly woke up to the feeling of a big hand on one of her breasts and a rather large erection pressing up against her ass. She realized that she'd wrapped her arm around Edward's waist at some point during the night and he was holding her hand in place with his. The feel of warm skin through the T-shirt she wore felt good. She was just surprised that Porter hadn't pulled his hand away when she'd pressed herself against Edward's back.

"I think she's awake now." Edward spoke softly into the early dawn morning.

"Hannah? You awake?" Porter asked softly next to her ear.

"Um, yeah. I was trying not to wake you two up," she confessed.

"Well, damn. I was really enjoying the feel of you, baby girl," Porter said with a chuckle.

"We don't have to get up right away, do we?" she asked.

"No right away, but soon," Edward said before he turned over, so that he was facing her.

To her surprise, he didn't jump away from where Porter's hand touched the skin of his chest. Instead, he smiled at her and lifted one hand to gently stroke her other nipple through her T-shirt. The sensation went straight to her pussy, sparking at her clit before causing her cunt walls to flutter in reaction. She closed her eyes at the spark that caught her by surprise.

"That feel good, honey?" Edward asked in a deep voice.

She shivered instead of answering him. Her tongue felt too heavy to work right then.

"I'd say that was a resounding yes, Edward. I want to taste them. Help me get her shirt off," Porter said scooting back slightly.

Hannah yelped when together, the two men whipped her T-shirt up and over her head despite her lying on it. It pulled from beneath her body and Edward tossed it off the bed.

"Aw, hell. Look at those beauties," Edward said before bending over and licking across the tip of one tit. "So pretty and tight for me. I love the color of them—dusky pink."

"Get her on her back. I want a taste," Porter said in a raspy voice.

She was carefully flipped to her back where she could barely make out the faces of both Porter and Edward leaning over her. Both men had their eyes plastered on her oversized breasts as if they couldn't drag them away. As much as she wanted this to work, the fact that both men were right there on top of her gave her a slight case of nerves. She knew what lay ahead at some point and was scared. Anal sex wasn't something she'd ever experienced before and despite the intense discussions and lectures on the subject, Hannah couldn't shake the fear that they would hurt her.

Edward looked up into her eyes as Porter closed his mouth around one nipple and sucked on it. Hot warm wetness surrounded it, as he drew on it. She couldn't stop her mouth from opening in a sigh or her eyes closing at the exquisite sensation.

The feel of hot breath at her earlobe had her opening her eyes once more.

"It's okay, honey. We'll take good care of you," he said in a soft whisper.

His mouth closed over her earlobe as he gently pulled and pinched her nipple. It wasn't enough. She needed more. They were being so careful with her, and though she wanted them to go slow, she didn't want them to go too slow.

"Please," she hissed out. The words she needed wouldn't come.

"Please what, baby girl?" Porter asked when he'd let go of her nipple.

Edward dropped his head to her breast and nipped at her nipple a little less carefully. She moaned in return. That was more like it.

"I think she wants a little more sensation than what we're giving her," Edward said.

"We're not going to hurt her," Porter said in that deep voice he had.

Just the sound of it grated across her nerve endings, exciting her so that her need ramped up even higher. That a man could turn her on with just his voice surprised her. She'd never met a man with a voice like Porter's though. It fairly dripped sex when he spoke like that. She was sure her pussy was wet already just from the little they'd done to her so far.

"I'd never hurt a woman, especially my woman," Edward said.

"Our woman," Porter countered.

"Let's take care of our woman." Edward returned to her torrid peak already hard and aching from his earlier nip.

She gasped when two sets of mouths latched on to her breast while their hands mounded her globes to the rhythm of their sucking and gentle biting. The more they played and tortured her tits, the closer she climbed up that steep hill that she'd only touched but never jumped off when with her past boyfriends. It had always taken her own hand to climax. They'd never been able to get her there.

Now, with these two men awakening fantasies she'd never known she'd had, Hannah couldn't help but wonder if just maybe she would finally have an orgasm that she hadn't provided herself. The wonder of that had her groaning with delight. The two men took her noises as a positive sign and Edward let go of the nipple he'd tended to and moved down her body, spreading hot wet kisses as he went.

Porter took over the other nipple with his fingers, pulling and pinching it just enough to have her clit pulsing with need. The feel of Edward between her legs, his face pressed against her soaked panties had her trying to pull back with embarrassment. He grabbed her hips to hold her still.

"Don't move, honey bear. I love the way you smell, all musky and hot." Edward's nose nudged the crotch of her panties.

She was sure her face was red as a balloon from how hot it felt. Why was he doing that? Did he really like smelling her when she was all hot and bothered?

"Is she wet, Edward?" Porter asked, his mouth hovering over her nipple.

"She's soaked, man. I love it. I've got to taste her."

Suddenly, Edward moved back and jerked her panties down her legs. He rolled over and pulled them off over her feet, tossing them behind him. Then he crawled slowly back up to slide between her thighs, pressing them farther apart in the process. His broad shoulders required her to spread them wide.

His hot breath fanned her wet pussy lips. He seemed to be just staring at her as he breathed her in. She wanted to see, but with Porter's head over her breasts, she couldn't see anything. Instead she had to wait for whatever came next. It had her on edge and anticipating. No doubt it was right where the two men wanted her.

The sudden touch of Edward's tongue along her pussy slit had her jerking her hips up in reaction. God that felt good! He retaliated by resting one hand on her pelvis and holding her down as he started licking up and down, delving between the wet folds to explore each crease before moving to the next one. His hot, wet mouth felt too good on her sex. She wanted to grind her crotch in his face. This wasn't like her. She'd never been this turned on or felt so sexy.

"Oh, God that feels so good! Please don't stop," she moaned.

Edward chuckled next to her pussy and the vibrations only added to her need. Then he circled her clit with the tip of his tongue and she nearly screamed at the intense pleasure that rippled through her body.

"Whatever you're doing down there, keep it up. She's panting up here. I'd say she's close to coming," Porter said with a smile in his voice.

Edward chuckled again against her clit. Hannah thought she would explode right then, but nothing prepared her for the man to suck her clit into his hot mouth and tongue it. White hot electricity shot from her throbbing clit to her cunt and on up to her nipples. The next nip of Porter's teeth on the swollen nub had her nearly screaming with pleasure.

"Oh, God, oh God, oh God." She couldn't think, couldn't breathe around the overwhelming emotion clogging her brain. What were they doing to her?

Edward slipped a finger between her folds to sink into her quivering cunt. He sucked hard on her clit as he added a second finger and fucked her with them as he drew on the throbbing bundle of nerves in his mouth. The sensation was too much. Hannah exploded around him, crying out as wave after wave of pleasure poured over her.

"That's it, baby girl. Ride it out," Porter whispered next to her ear as he pulled and pinched on both nipples. "We've got you. Enjoy it, Hannah."

Enjoy was too tame of a word for what she did. She rode a white hot wave of sensation that drove her to the ends of existence. She could only hold on lest she fall off and lose herself forever. Nothing could ever top this. She'd been missing out on a lot of feel good in her life. Not anymore. These two men had given her something she'd never even imagined. She'd make damn sure she took good care of them so they would never regret keeping her.

Chapter Four

Porter released his hold on Hannah's nipples as she slowly collapsed against him. He couldn't stop the pleased smile that took over his mouth. They'd given her a damn good orgasm. He hoped it was more than she'd ever felt before. Keeping her happy was important since she had such a difficult road ahead of her.

Besides taking care of two men and keeping them sexually satisfied, she had the house and a garden to tend to and then there would be children eventually. Cam and Phillip had told them that they now made sure that at least one man was always close in case of problems among their group of farmers and when their wife got to be rather far along in pregnancy, one of them would always be with her in case she had trouble. It made him feel a little better but not a lot.

"I've got to get inside of you, Hannah. I'm so fucking hard I'm going to blow as soon as I do though," Edward said, jostling Porter back from his thoughts.

"Hannah. I want you to suck my cock, baby girl. Can you do that for me?" he asked.

God, if she didn't want to suck him off, he'd die of need before he could get inside of her. She'd need to rest before she would be able to take another fucking.

Instead of answering him, their woman opened her mouth, her sweet hazel eyes smiling up at him. Peace settled over him as he scrambled out of his pajama bottoms to kneel on the bed next to her head. With one hand on the headboard, he guided his throbbing shaft to her plump kissable lips. Her pink tongue reached out and licked over the crown sending tingles all down the shaft of his dick. Then she licked at the slit at the top as if trying to get more of the liquid that had leaked out.

"Hell, baby girl. That feels too good. Suck my dick, Hannah," he rasped out, resisting the urge to pull her hair until she took him into her hot mouth.

She moaned around him when she took just his cockhead into her wet mouth. The vibrations shot straight to his aching balls, making him lunge forward slightly, sinking another good inch between her lips. She didn't gag or pull back at the sudden intrusion. Instead, she tightened her lips around him and sucked hard on his thick rod.

He pried his eyes open to see Edward sinking balls deep into their woman's pussy. The other man looked as if he was in heaven with her wrapped around his cock. He opened his eyes and smiled at Porter. Then he pulled out until he was almost all the way out of her before plunging deep once more.

Hannah screamed around him, digging her fingers into one hip and one ass cheek. He nearly shot his load at the way her scream vibrated not only his dick but also his balls. She reached between his legs with the hand that had been on his hip and fondled his balls. The feel of her hands on his nuts had him groaning. She squeezed them gently then plucked on the skin between them.

"Yeah, just like that." Porter had to grit his teeth not to dig his fingers into her scalp, but it didn't stop him from threading them through her hair.

She scraped her teeth lightly down his shaft as she carefully scratched her nails over his balls. The more she took of him, the harder it got to hold back. She was testing his restraint to the max. The way her tongue wound around his cock as she took him to the back of her throat had him aching to release, but he didn't want to come so soon. He felt like a teenager who hadn't learned how to control himself with a woman. Every move of her mouth over his shaft had him fighting the need to release.

"Aw, hell your mouth is so damn hot," he managed to croak out.

"Fuck, she's tight! I'm not going to last near long enough," Edward ground out as he fucked her.

Porter groaned when she suddenly swallowed around him. The feel of her throat muscles contracting down around his dick had his balls drawing up, his cum boiling to release. If she kept doing that he wouldn't last.

He tried to distract her by massaging her scalp with his fingers without pulling on her hair. He wanted to fuck her mouth, but was scared he would frighten her or choke her. He had no idea how much experience she'd had giving head, but at that moment, it felt as if she was an expert.

Her moans vibrated against his dick as she sucked on just the crown, running the tip of her tongue all along the slit in it. Porter growled at the intense pleasure she was giving him.

Every stroke of her mouth down his shaft felt like pure heaven. Each time she pulled off of him he swore. The need to come pulsed in his shaft and tightened his balls.

Hannah took him to the back of her throat then just a little deeper and swallowed around him as she groaned. That extra little bit was the last straw. He hollered out her name as cum erupted from his cock into her mouth and throat. She swallowed convulsively around him stimulating even more cum from his balls. He swore she drained him by the time he had finished coming. She slowly backed off of him, panting and moaning with Edward's cock riding her fast and hard.

Porter leaned against the wall on one hand as his other one caressed her head. She'd drained him of more than just his seed. The woman had zapped him of energy as well. There was no way in hell he would be able to get out of bed now. He needed another nap. His ass cheeks ached from clenching them as he'd emptied his balls with his climax. What in the hell was he going to do when he finally got in her sweet ass?

* * * *

Hannah thought she'd go insane with how good it felt for Edward to be inside of her. She'd imagined it would be over in seconds and she would be left wanting, but not only had they taken care of her first, Edward was dragging out her pleasure to the point that she wanted to scream for him to let her come already. The man had said he wouldn't last, but hell how long could he go?

His dick stretched her so good. It rubbed over that sweet spot almost every stroke and when he pulled all the way out and plunged back in, it was almost more than she could take. It felt amazing.

"I want to hear you scream when you come again, Hannah. No one is close enough to hear it but us," Edward said in a near growl.

He reached between them and stroked her clit as he thrust inside of her. The combination was more than she could take. Stars exploded behind her eyes as she squeezed them shut. Pleasure stronger even than earlier detonated in her cunt. The warm waves of ecstasy spread out in swirls of sensation unlike anything she'd ever felt before. The scream that left he mouth didn't even sound like her.

"Fuck! I'm coming, Hannah. Oh, hell that feels amazing," Edward called out.

Hannah's body convulsed as she shot to heaven, zinging by thousands of stars on the way. There was no way she'd be able to function after this. Her body was a molten mess, a puddle of nerves. How had she missed experiencing this? Was it just that there were two of them or were they both so skilled that she hadn't had a chance?

Edward collapsed over her but managed to keep from crushing her as he shifted so that most of his weight was on his side. He stroked her damp skin with callused fingers.

Porter sank down on the other side of her, curling into her with one hand splayed out over her tummy. Edward slowly pulled from her quivering pussy and slid closer to her as well. She couldn't seem to stop panting, but then Edward was breathing hard as well. Porter seemed to have caught his breath and was actually snoring next to her. She couldn't hold in the giggle.

"What are you laughing at?" Edward asked.

"Porter is snoring. I think he needed a nap," she said.

"Sounds like a pretty damn good idea to me, too." Edward dropped his hand just above Porter's and sighed as he closed his eyes.

Hannah had to hold in another bout of giggles as Edward almost immediately fell asleep as well. She wasn't the least bit tired. In fact, she felt energized. She wanted to get up and explore the house some more while it was daylight. She knew she couldn't go outside yet, but could look out the windows to see what was around them.

Instead, she lay there between the two men just enjoying their touch and the warmth of their bodies. She'd never dreamed she would have a husband with how the world had started to fall apart. Now she had not one, but two men in her life. Learning how to please them and keep them happy would be a big endeavor, but she vowed to keep them happy. They'd sure made her happy.

After a good thirty minutes of soaking up the feel of them surrounding her, Hannah slipped from between them and crawled off the foot of the bed. She cleaned up and got dressed in the bathroom so as not to wake them. Then she hurried downstairs to find out more about the house and the world they lived on.

The view from the kitchen windows showed that a fence surrounded a large area of land. She imagined most of it would be taken up with the garden. They would have to get started on it right away. There were two trees near the back of the fenced in areas. One was an amazing blue with lighter blue leaves. The other one had swirls of green and orange. The leaves didn't look like anything she'd ever seen before either. Instead of flat, they looked almost like feathers that floated in the wind.

The grass was a much deeper color as well. It looked dark blue and seemed thick like carpet. The occasional flower rose up from the sea of waving strands. She'd learned on the shuttle that some of the flowers were poisonous. She would need to consult her pamphlets to tell which were which.

The next thing she did was look around the kitchen a little closer. There was plenty of cabinets and counter space. She liked that they had the kitchen table and chairs right there instead of a separate dining room. The mudroom where the washer and dryer combo stood had a sink as well. She checked the pantry and found that it was a nice size. Inside the pantry was the door to the basement. She started to open the door and go down to check it out, but remembered that the guys had said they hadn't looked at it yet. She didn't want to find any surprises. She could wait until they had cleared it first.

Instead, Hannah explored the living room. There wasn't a TV, of course, but there were bookshelves and a few books. They looked a little empty surrounding the fireplace, but maybe they would find something else to fill them eventually. The two leather lounge chairs looked comfortable as did the couch and rocking chair. On the other side of the fireplace and off the entrance area was the office. She looked in and found that there were two desks, a long table that held the radio equipment, and a file cabinet.

When she walked out of the office and across the living room, she heard noises from upstairs and figured the men were awake. She hurried to the kitchen and started breakfast. They would be hungry and ready to eat when they made it down. Hannah didn't want them to have to wait on their food.

"Hannah! Where are you?" Edward's voice sang out as he bounded down the stairs.

"I'm in the kitchen. Breakfast will be ready in a few minutes," she called back.

He'd sounded almost panicked. Had he worried that she'd go outside? She wasn't an idiot. She frowned and refrained from looking over when she heard one of them walk into the room.

Large hands settled on her waist. By their size, she knew they belonged to Edward. While his were big, Porter's were much larger.

"Hungry?" she asked as she scooped the eggs from the pan onto a plate.

"For more than food, though," he said in a gruff voice.

She laughed. "You just had me, silly."

"I may never get enough of being inside of you. You're addicting, honey."

She could feel her skin heat at his words. After the rough start they'd gotten, she hadn't expected him to be so loving so soon. It felt good.

"Something smells good." Porter's deeper voice called from the other room.

"She's cooking breakfast. Looks about ready, too," Edward called back.

She turned from the stove with the plate of eggs, but Edward took them from her. He carried them over to the table and set them down before returning to take the other plates from her as well.

"I'll get the juice from the fridge," she said.

When she returned to the table, both men were sitting down waiting on her. She poured juice into each glass then sat down and began passing the plates of food.

"What are you planning to do today? When do you start working?" she asked.

"We're going to look around the fenced in area and start plowing the garden," Edward said.

"We don't start working until the garden is plowed and planted. I figure it will take us three days to do all of that," Porter said, forking up some eggs. "We've also got to check the basement and out buildings. There's supposed to be some sort of cart you can use to go back and forth to see Cam and Phillip's wife, Lacy. I want to make sure it's working well. It's solar operated. It has an enclosed cab so you should be safe from most of the animal life out here."

"Do you know how to shoot a gun, Hannah?" Edward asked.

"No. I've never even held one before," she admitted.

"You're going to need to be able to hear. If we aren't around, you need to be able to defend yourself from the creatures," he said.

"I'll learn. I'm not shy about trying new things," she said.

The two men exchanged glances then burst out laughing. She frowned then thought back over what she'd said and smiled as well. Hannah had a feeling that she'd be trying a lot of new things before it was over with.

They talked about the farming methods they used on Alpha and how with the two moons at night, the plants seemed to grow even faster than on Earth. The conversation they'd had with the other men the night before had revealed that there were a lot of things they would need to get used to.

"Cam said the summers are hot but nice while the winters are bitterly cold. He said the thunderstorms can be pretty intense, so we don't need to be outside in them." Edward sat back from the table and stretched.

"I love thunderstorms, but I will stay out of them here. I've seen and read enough about Alpha to know that things are much different than they were on Earth," she told him.

"You can say that again. They want us to come over for dinner one night before we start work to talk about some of the changes," Porter told her. "They said not everything has been shared with people back on Earth. That makes me a little nervous."

Hannah could agree with that. It made her nervous to think that there were things that they didn't know about yet. That suggested that they were bad and that scared her since there were plenty of bad things about Alpha already. She didn't want to think that there were other things to worry about.

"As soon as we get the garden going, we'll go see what more there is to know," Porter continued.

"Do you think we need to know before we start working outside?" she asked.

"They assured us we were okay as long as we stayed in the fence and kept watch around us. They said all of the dangerous plants had been removed, but to start watching for them to reappear in the next week," Edward said.

"We need to get started, Edward. We got a little distracted in bed this morning." Porter winked at Hannah.

She could feel the heat burn up her neck and face at his teasing. That seemed to amuse Edward since he started chuckling. She just stood up and started gathering dishes.

"We'll help you clear the table, baby girl. Then we're going to check out the basement and explore outside some. You stay inside for now." Porter grabbed his plate and utensils as he stood up.

She watched with surprise as both men took their plates and glasses to the sink. She'd never known men who didn't mind helping some in the kitchen. She vowed once more to make sure she made them happy. Nothing could have surprised her more than to have ended up with two amazing and generous men like Edward and Porter. She was thankful Edward had given her a chance. She wouldn't allow him to regret it. She might have started out on the wrong leg with him, but he was letting her make things right, and that meant more to her than anything except maybe knowing her sister was safe.

The brief thought of her sister had her blinking back tears, wishing she knew for sure her sister was safe and happy. She prayed that somehow, her sister would end up being allowed to travel to another planet where she had the chance at being safe and cared for. It was the only other prayer she had now that she was doing so well with her two men.

Her two men. Hannah still had to remind herself that it was true. She was with two men and they treated her like a princess so far. Alpha was going to be a good place no matter what she had to do to make it so.

Porter and Edward both dropped a quick kiss to her lips before grabbing their rifles and heading down to the basement. Worry tightened her throat, but Hannah trusted that they could take care of themselves and turned to wash up the dishes while they made sure the basement was safe. Then she wanted to see what was down there so she could plan the garden and be sure she had plenty of jars for canning.

The sound of the two men talking and laughing loosened the knot in her throat. They sounded like they got along well. She wished she knew more about them. Maybe they could talk more after dinner that night. How had they met and did they know each other before being paired? So many things to learn and a new life in which to do it. Hannah had much to be thankful for.

Chapter Five

"What do you think? Is this going to give us enough gardening room? Cam's measurements seemed a bit small to me. We need to be able to eat out of this for a full year until the next growing season," Porter said.

"I agree. I think adding the extra fifteen square feet should be enough though. They assured us that the soil here produced much more than we were used to on Earth. We've got to trust that they won't tell us anything that will harm us. We're all here to help each other." Edward stood up from where he'd driven the last marking stake into the ground.

Porter sighed. He wanted to trust the other family, but trust wasn't easy with him when it came to competing farms. The fact that he wasn't competing with anyone else to sell his crops kept slipping his mind though. They were all working together to feed their family and the community as a whole. They didn't sell their crops or receive anything more than anyone else. As long as they all pulled their weight, they had equal access to whatever they needed.

"What's worrying you?" Edward asked frowning at him.

"I don't know. I guess I'm having trouble accepting that things are different here. It worries me to trust someone else to give us the information we need. Back on Earth we couldn't trust anyone or we ran the risk of losing our farms."

"I hear you, man, but it is different here. They need us as much as we need them. The only way anyone will survive here is by pulling together and helping each other," Edward said.

Porter looked out around them at the strange new sights surrounding them. A lot had changed from the first pictures they'd been shown while on the shuttle. New families didn't have to put up their own fences anymore. Everything was set up for them from the start with the exception of starting a garden. They'd found that it saved time and prevented accidents from happening when there was already a fence in place.

There were five carpenter families on Alpha now that shared the work of building new homes. The supply ships from Earth arrived every three months bringing partially constructed housing now along with the last of Earth's stores of supplies for them to manufacture their own things. It looked as if there would only be another few years before the Earth's sun destroyed what was left of their original home. He didn't think the women knew this since Hannah still hoped her sister might have a chance at a normal life. He wouldn't be telling her about it either.

"Ready to start plowing?" Edward asked.

"Yeah. We need to get this ready for planting as soon as possible. You want to start off on the tractor?" Porter asked.

"Yeah. You keep watch while I get it started." Edward strode toward the barn like structure where their equipment was stored. The back side was open to the fenced in area while the front side had a door that stayed latched.

Porter watched as Edward used the battery start up then drove the tractor out into the sunshine where the solar panels would convert the sun's rays to power the tractor. When he started turning the earth, Porter kept vigil with the rifle cradled in his arms like a child.

Several times he noticed small animals that resembled a dog poking their heads up several yards on the other side of the fence, but they didn't attempt to venture closer or stay long. Porter didn't trust that they wouldn't try and sneak closer, so he made frequent passes near the fence line checking the area. Phillip had warned them to watch for holes being dug under the fences. The thought of one of them getting under the fence to attack Hannah worried him. He planned to make sure she learned how to shoot as soon as possible.

After nearly two hours of plowing, Edward stopped the tractor at the end of one row and climbed off the machine to stretch. Porter walked over to see how he was doing.

"Need a break?" he asked the other man.

"Yeah. I'm going to grab a drink. Do you want something?"

"I'm fine. I'll go ahead and take over the plow." Porter handed off the rifle and walked toward the tractor. "Oh, there've been some of those dog things out there watching, but they don't get very close."

Edward grunted but nodded and turned to head for the backdoor to the house. It was obvious to Porter that the other man was a bit stiff by the way he limped as he walked. Neither one of them had gotten much exercise while on the shuttle. Instead, they'd been learning about the planet and how to survive.

One he'd climbed up on the plow, Porter started it and resumed plowing their garden. He figured another four or five passes over it and it would be ready to row up for planting. He doubted they would get it rowed before night fall even with the extra hour in the day. Still, considering everything they'd done and the late start they'd gotten, Porter was happy with their progress.

He realized it had been a few minutes since Edward had gone inside for that drink and wondered if something was wrong. Then he smiled to himself. If he'd been Edward, he'd have taken advantage of having a few minutes alone with their woman. No doubt that was what his partner was doing right then. A little envy broke through, but to his relief, true jealousy didn't rear its head at the thought of the other man with Hannah. Porter felt only relief that he didn't have to shoulder all the burden of keeping her safe among the dangers that Alpha provided. Hannah would be kept safe.

* * * *

Hannah heard the back door open then close and figured one of the men had come inside to get something to drink. She left the book she'd been reading about the first years on Alpha that someone had put together and went in search of whichever man had come inside. She nearly screamed when Edward walked into the living room as she rounded the corner from the office.

"Goodness. You startled me. Is everything okay?" she asked looking to see if Porter had come in with him.

"It's going well. The garden will be ready to row up tomorrow and plant by tomorrow afternoon." Edward wrapped his arms around her and pulled her in close. "What have you been up to?"

"I was reading that book about what life has been like here so far. It was on one of the desks and I thought it would help me be better prepared if I knew more about what to expect."

"Good idea. How are you feeling this afternoon?"

Hannah wasn't sure what he meant. "I'm fine."

He chuckled. "Not too sore?"

She felt her skin warm at the reference to their morning romp. She could only shake her head, her throat too clogged with embarrassment to say anything.

"I really want a taste of that sweet pussy, honey." He backed her slowly toward the couch. "Think I could sneak a taste before going back outside?"

"Uh, I…" She didn't know what to say. The arm of the couch hit her right below the ass and she nearly fell backward.

"Easy there, sweet thing." Edward went to his knees in front of her and unfastened her pants, watching her face the entire time he undressed her. She could tell he was trying not to frighten her, but she wasn't scared, just surprised.

"You taste so sweet, Hannah. I'll make you feel real good, honey," he said as he helped her out of her shoes and then her pants and panties. "I'm going to talk to Porter about making it a rule that you can't wear panties when we're around. It takes too long to get you naked."

She couldn't stop the chuckle that escaped and put her hand over her mouth when it did. The expression on Edward's face once she was naked from the waist down had her drawing in a deep breath. Hunger wild and deep darkened his light blue eyes. He closed his eyes and drew in a deep breath before standing back up and lifting her so that her ass rested on the arm of the couch.

"Don't move, honey. I don't want you to fall."

"Fall?" She asked then gasped as he went back to his knees and spread her legs, lifting them over his shoulders.

The movement threw her back against the seat cushions of the couch with her butt still resting on the arm. She was spread wide open to him with her legs over his shoulders. This position had her pussy front and center to his intense gaze leaving her unable to move away.

"What are you doing?"

"Getting my little taste of heaven, Hannah," he said just before he buried his face against her pussy and growled.

The vibrations against her clit had her squeezing her own eyes shut for a second at the amazing sensations tingling over the bundle of nerves. Then he licked her slit with long slow swipes of his tongue, teasing her folds before lapping again. He groaned as if in pain, but Hannah doubted that was the reason behind the sensuous sound.

His fingers were kneading her inner thighs like a kitten. One hand moved away and she gasped as he inserted two fingers just inside her wet opening. She couldn't believe she was lying over the couch while he ravished her like this. What about Porter? Would he be upset if he found out what Edward was doing to her? There wasn't supposed to be any jealousy, but they didn't know each other very well yet.

"Your pussy tastes better than candy, Hannah. I could feast on you and not get enough of how you taste," Edward said around another groan.

He pressed his two fingers in deeper then pulled them out slowly. Over and over he sank them deeper inside of her until he was all the way up to his knuckles inside her cunt. When he moved them around inside of her, brushing over sensitive spots, Hannah hissed out a loud "*yes*," causing him to stop and stroke that spot again and again.

"Right there, honey? Does that feel good?" he asked.

She couldn't answer him when he sucked on her clit at the same time his busy fingers rasped over that sweet spot inside her cunt. Pleasure bloomed fast, spreading out from her abdomen through her bloodstream to include every inch of her body. It felt like warm chocolate syrup pouring over her body, encasing her in sinfully decadent pleasure. She never wanted to move from that spot.

"I take it that felt good," Edward said with a chuckle. "I bet Porter knows what we're up to in here. What do you think?"

"Oh, my, God! I was that loud? Is he going to be mad? I don't want him to get mad at us." She tried to reach up to him so she could get off the couch.

When he didn't take her hand to help her sit up, she tried to roll over so she could roll off the couch. His hand shot out that time but only to hold her firmly in place.

"I told you to be still so you wouldn't fall, Hannah. Don't worry about Porter. He isn't going to be upset. We're all three together now. We're each going to want some alone time with you once in a while." Edward frowned down at her. "You don't need to worry about upsetting us. We'll work things out between us. It's not your concern."

She started to interrupt him, but the sight of him unfastening his jeans left her with her mouth hanging open. He was going to screw her right then and there. From the looks of his dick, he'd been as turned on by the oral sex as she'd been. He was swollen and throbbing as he lowered his pants letting his cock free.

"Like what you see, honey? It's all yours," he said with a grin.

Hannah closed her mouth and relaxed back against the cushions once again. Her belly ached from her attempts to raise herself up despite being unbalanced on the couch's arm. Edward lowered himself over her, placing his hands on either side of her head. The focused look he gave her left no doubt as to his intentions. He planned to ravish her better than any of the historical rakes she'd read about in her books.

She watched as he slowly lowered his head until he was barely a whisper away from her. His lips brushed hers then he nipped her lower lip before she felt the press of his cockhead against her pussy. He nipped again then buried his face against her neck as he pressed forward with a deep groan.

"So good. So fucking good, honey," he said in a muffled voice.

All Hannah could manage was a sigh as he slipped deeper inside of her. She'd never thought of herself as particularly sexual, but Edward and Porter made her feel sexy and needy all at the same time. She liked how she felt when they touched her. How could she feel this way after knowing them less than a day?

"What is it, Hannah? Am I hurting you?" Edward started to pull back from her.

She wrapped her arms around his neck to keep him there. "No! I'm confused, I guess. How can I feel this good with both of you when I don't even know you yet?"

"We're your men, honey. It's okay to feel that way with us. There's nothing wrong with wanting us as much as we want you," he said, looking into her eyes. "We'll get to know each other better over time. Right now, we're sexually attracted to each other and that's a good thing."

She liked to see him smile. He hadn't smiled when she'd first met him at the station, but then there had been the fact that she'd replaced their true wife. She didn't want to think about that anymore. They were hers and she was theirs now. That was all that mattered. She pulled him down and kissed him.

Her kiss must have been what he needed to know that she was okay. He plunged into her cunt with one swift shift of his hips and all other thoughts flew out of her head. He felt so good inside of her.

Edward watched her face as he thrust in and out of her in slow deep strokes. She wrapped her legs around his waist and lifted her hips to meet each drive of his cock deep into her pussy. Hannah couldn't say anything, her voice frozen with emotion. She'd never connected to anyone like she was to Edward right then. His eyes told her how much he enjoyed what they were doing, but they also told her she mattered. She felt him touch her all the way to her soul.

Pleasure built once again as he slowly increased his strokes until they were both sweating and gasping for breath. His intense stare held her gaze until her orgasm took her away, and she squeezed her eyes shut as she called out his name and soared. She dimly heard him shout hers a few seconds later and felt the heated pulses of his cum filling her.

When she opened her eyes again, it was to find his head thrown back with his eyes squeezed shut, enjoying his last tremors of release. Then he opened them and smiled.

"Just what a man needs after a day's work, honey. Thanks." He slowly pulled from her and helped her sit up on the arm of the couch.

"Um, I don't think you've had a full day's work yet, though," she said with a shy smile.

He chuckled. "I expect Porter will agree with you on that. I better hurry on out there before he comes hunting me."

Before she could do it herself, Edward knelt and started putting her clothes back on her. She felt embarrassed now that the heat of the moment and all had passed. She started to walk away once she was dressed, but he pulled her into his arms and kissed her soundly on the lips.

"Thanks, Hannah. We'll be back inside for dinner in a few hours." Edward released her and walked toward the kitchen to go out the back door.

Hannah touched her fingers to her lips, savoring the kiss for a brief moment. To her, that kiss was so much more than it would have been before their tryst. They shared something more than just sex that time. She felt a little better about their relationship now. She hoped he was on the way to forgiving her for her deception now because Hannah could see herself falling in love with him very easily. Love him while he carried a grudge would break her heart and just might break her spirit as well.

Chapter Six

"Looks like we've got it all planted, baby girl. You've worked hard today," Porter said, wiping his arm across his forehead.

"I can't believe how fast it went with all three of us working on it. Now all I have to do is keep it watered and weeded. I still can't believe it will grow as fast as they say it will. Doesn't seem possible," she said picking up the empty packets of seeds. "I'll pick up out here then clean up and start dinner."

"Why don't we all pick up and go get a shower? Then we can each make our own sandwiches tonight. I think we all deserve a rest," Edward said, dropping a kiss on her nose.

"Sounds good to me." Porter followed Edward as they took the garden tools to the doors leading down to the basement.

Hannah watched them and found herself thinking about that morning when they'd made love to her before getting up. She couldn't believe how giving they were. Men weren't usually so sensitive to a woman's needs. She hoped it would last long enough for her to get used to them and their relationship. Learning to live with two men wasn't easy to do. Plus, they'd gotten started out on the wrong foot to begin with. Feeling comfortable with her place in their lives still hadn't happened for her yet.

She carried the empty see sacks to the cellar where they would store them until they needed to obtain more seeds next year. Nothing was wasted. Anything that couldn't be reused was turned into fuel for winter.

Just as she reached the steps to the cellar, Porter climbed up and took her burden. He smiled and turned away to carry the box of empty seed bags down. That left her with nothing more to do except go inside. Hannah hurried to the back door and raced inside to make it to the shower before the guys made it. She wanted to at least rinse off before one or both of them joined her. She felt as if she had dirt caked on her skin like a second layer.

The warm water felt great as she stepped into it and plunged her head under the pulsing stream. By the time the men arrived, she'd actually finished washing up and was shampooing her hair.

"What took you so long?" she asked in a teasing voice.

"Heard the radio when we walked inside and stopped to talk to Cam and Phillip. They want us to come over tomorrow around lunch time to visit and talk," Edward said as he stepped in behind her.

Immediately nerves began to jumble her stomach. She froze for a second with her hands in her hair and shampoo sliding down her face.

"Whoa there, honey. You're getting shampoo in your eyes. Let's get you rinsed off before you burn them." Edward urged her beneath the spray and proceeded to rinse her hair, making sure she got all of the soap off her face.

"Thanks," she managed to say before stepping out of the shower.

He let her go seeming not to have notice anything was wrong. She wasn't as lucky with Porter though. He wrapped a towel around her head before gently patting her skin with another.

"What's wrong, baby girl? I can tell something is up."

She licked her lips. "I'm just nervous about meeting the others. I mean what's going to happen when you introduce me as Hannah and not Gladys?"

He froze this time then he shrugged. "Nothing. I doubt they even knew who was going to be our wife. They probably only knew that they were getting more help with the crops. I don't want you worrying about it. Okay?"

She nodded, but Hannah couldn't just forget. Now she had all night to worry. The one thing she was looking forward to was learning more about the planet and seeing their daughter, Julie who was two. It would be nice to be friends with Lacy since they would be so close to each other. She knew that another farming family lived on the other side of them. She didn't know how often she would see them though. She wasn't sure if they had a child or not.

As she dressed to go downstairs to make a sandwich, Edward got out of the shower and Porter stepped in. She couldn't stop herself from watching as her men moved completely comfortable being nude around her. Both of them were amazing to look at. She had to make herself finish and head downstairs.

"I'll be there to help in a minute, honey," Edward called out.

Hannah hurried downstairs to pull out all the ingredients for sandwiches. She wasn't very hungry anymore. Anticipating what might happen the following day was enough to leave her tummy rolling.

"You didn't have to wait on us to fix yourself something to eat, honey." Edward's voice startled her.

"I'm not really hungry. I was thinking about eating some of the fresh fruit since it won't last much longer." She walked back to the counter and picked up an apple and rinsed it in the sink before sitting down at the table.

She'd already poured some of the posco tea that she'd made up that morning. It wasn't her favorite, but she hadn't made any of the stone berry lemonade yet. She would do that in the morning. Since they had requested the tea that was what she'd made.

Taking a sip from her glass, she looked up to see Edward watching her as he made his sandwiches. She had a feeling he was just waiting on Porter to make it down before he said something about her not eating. She couldn't help it if she wasn't hungry anymore.

Great. Now I'm pouting like a child. I've got to settle down and stop obsessing over the fact that I took another woman's place in their lives. I made the decision and it's done.

Hannah needed to move on. They obviously had. It was only an issue because she kept it alive. She was sure she was in for a talking to once Porter made it to the table.

Sure enough, the second Porter sat down and started making his sandwiches, Edward pointed out that she wasn't eating.

"What's wrong, baby girl?" Porter asked setting down the knife.

"Nothing. I'm just not real hungry. Besides, the fruit will ruin if we don't eat it and you weren't too thrilled with it for breakfast this morning," she pointed out.

"Don't confuse the issue, honey." Edward frowned at her. "That's not enough to keep you going after all the work you've done today."

"He's right. Are you sick? Do you feel bad?" Porter asked.

"No. I'm not ill. I'm just nervous about tomorrow." She realized they weren't going to let it go.

"Hannah, honey. You don't have any reason to be nervous. They're our neighbors. They just want to meet us and tell us more about Alpha and what to expect. It's going to be a lot easier on us than it was for them because they didn't have anyone to warn them. Relax and stop worrying about it." Edward reached out and brushed her hair behind her ear.

"Okay. I'm trying." She still didn't reach for the sliced bread. She couldn't force herself to eat.

Both men went back to their sandwiches and as soon as they were finished eating, Hannah jumped up and began cleaning up. They each kissed her lightly on the cheek before leaving her alone in the kitchen. She figured they would hole up in the office for a while to look at the information they had about the farming they would be responsible for. She hoped they were right and no one would say anything about her name not being Gladys. She'd die of embarrassment if anything was said about it.

Hannah was dead on her feet by the time she'd tidied up the kitchen and set things out for breakfast in the morning. She figured she would head up to bed early. They guys might be in the office for another couple of hours but she just didn't think she could sit up that long.

When she walked into the bedroom, she nearly screamed to find both men sitting up in bed waiting on her.

* * * *

Porter smiled at the shock on Hannah's face. She had figured they were in the office working. Edward had been right. Waiting on her to come to bed had been a good idea. She needed some distraction and he was onboard with using sex to distract her. Making love to his woman would always be at the top of his favorite things to do. She was perfect in more ways than one. Her honey colored hair was a silky temptation in itself. He longed to feel it brush over his cock. Hell, as sick as it sounded, he would love to stroke himself with it until he came.

Then there were her amazing hazel eyes. The green fractals that broke up the soft browns captured his attention whenever he held her, which wasn't nearly often enough. Right now he watched as she regained her composure and studied them. He could almost see her trying to decide what to do. Edward, ever the outspoken one, decided for her.

"Don't just stand there, woman. Get naked and climb into bed. We've been waiting on you forever. Sharing a bed with you and Porter is fine, but I don't much care to sit up here without clothes on next to him for nearly an hour."

She giggled then started pulling off her clothes. When she was down to her underwear, he noticed how she hesitated before finally removing the last pieces. Instead of walking over to one of them to get in next to them, Hannah chose to climb up from the foot of the bed between them. Seeing her ass twitch as she crawled had his dick twitching in anticipation of playing with her some tonight.

"Climb up here on top of me, honey. I want to taste those sweet tits of yours. I've been thinking about how pretty they are all day long," Edward said, reaching for her.

Edward scooted down in the bed so that he was prone with his head on one pillow. When Hannah's face reached his, his partner pulled her head down for a kiss. The way she moaned when he took her mouth made him smile. He loved hearing her moan even if it was because of something Edward was doing. She'd moan for him soon enough.

"Okay, move on up, honey. Keep that ass in the air for Porter. He wants a taste of your sweet syrup while I suck on this nipples. Look how hard they are." Edward pulled lightly on one of them as she crawled higher up his body. "Right there, honey."

Porter waited until Hannah was caught up in Edward sucking and plucking on her ripe nipples before he moved behind her to the foot of the bed. When he pushed her thighs farther apart, she stiffened for a second but quickly complied. He could see nearly every inch of her sweet pussy and tight little puckered star. His mouth watered at the thought of tonging her clit and lapping up every drop of her juices.

As soon as he touched her slit with the tip of his tongue, Hannah moaned for him. It was music to his ears. He licked her up and down then teased her clit by circling all around it without actually running his tongue over the top. She tried to move with him, but he held her hips still so she couldn't control his attentions. He wanted her wild to climax, the need to come so intense that she wouldn't notice as much when he played with her back hole. They hadn't touched her there yet, wanting to allow her time to get used to them a bit more.

As he held her still for his mouth to play with her, Porter breathed her unique scent in. He loved the way she smelled, all earthy and musky at the same time. He couldn't wait for her to come so he could bury his face there and lap at her juices.

"You like a little pinch now and then, honey?" Edward asked.

Porter stilled, unsure if he liked what Edward seemed to be doing. She was their woman, their wife as far as he was concerned. He didn't want her to ever feel pain or discomfort.

"God, yes. That feels so good," she said.

He relaxed some when he realized she'd grown even wetter from Porter's play. If she truly enjoyed the slight pain, he wanted her to have what she needed. He growled as he lapped at her growing arousal. From the way she was soaking his tongue, she was ready for more.

"You taste like spicy candy, baby girl. I could lick your honey for hours and not get tired."

He teased her clit with a soft kiss then ran the tip of one finger up and down her slit before entering her to his first knuckle. She groaned, his cock jumping at the sound. When he withdrew it, she whimpered. He thrust it back inside her until he was all the way to his hand and wiggled it. Her cunt rippled across it, letting him know she wanted more. Porter loved knowing he could make her feel good, loved the feeling of importance it gave him. Making her feel good thrilled him.

When he added a second finger, Porter slowly pushed inside of her as he lightly tweaked her clit with his tongue over and over. The loud moan and wiggle of her ass told him she enjoyed it.

"Whatever you're doing back there has her nipples hard as diamonds up here. I'm going to break a damn tooth on them," Porter said with a soft chuckle. "Damn, she's hot!"

"I might not ever let you get a chance down here again, man. I love the taste of her," Porter told him.

"Don't you worry. I'll have my taste if I have to sneak home for a nooner now and then."

"Oh, God, please! Someone do something. I'm so close." Hannah's plea had them both chuckling but they stopped talking and returned to giving her pleasure.

Porter sucked on her clit until she was on the verge of exploding around him. He stopped and dragged his fingers from her cunt back to her ass where he circled the little puckered hole with them. He painted them with her own juices then added more before slowly breaching her with one finger as he filled her pussy with two fingers from his other hand. She stiffened for a split second but relaxed just as quickly. It didn't seem to bother her too much when he slowly worked his finger in and out of her back hole.

The way she moaned and moved a little with him made Porter believe she was already enjoying it, but he didn't want to assume anything. He continued to stroke her pussy with his other fingers as well. Then, when she seemed ready, he added more of her liquid and added a second finger to her ass.

"Press out for me, baby girl. Just like that. Relax for me," he said as he managed to enter her with both fingers. "That's it, sweet Hannah."

She moaned and began rocking with him as he fucked her with both sets of fingers. Two in her pussy and two in her ass.

"Yes! I'm so close. Please, let me come," she whimpered.

"Come for us honey," Edward urged.

Porter removed the fingers from her cunt and gently squeezed her clit several times as he continued to work her ass with the other fingers. Her scream alone told him she'd climaxed, but the feel of her ass milking his fingers told him even more. Their woman loved having her ass filled. He couldn't wait to take her there.

"Edward. She's ready."

"You're sure?" he asked looking over a collapsed Hannah's shoulder at him.

"Yeah. I'd never hurt her."

The other man nodded and continued to rub his hand up and down her back as she shivered over him. He slowly removed his fingers from her and hurried to the bathroom to clean up and grab some of the natural lube they'd been stocked with. It was made from one of the plants on Alpha.

When he returned, Edward had Hannah sitting up again but now she was straddling his lap. Judging by the aroused expression on her face, she was riding his partner's cock. Edward hadn't wasted any time. That suited him just fine. His dick felt like a damn tree truck between his legs as he walked. If he got any harder, he might actually break off when he did get inside of her.

Porter slowly caressed her ass cheeks, marveling at how smooth and soft she was. He squeezed them then pulled them apart to dribble the lubricating liquid down her crack. He added a generous amount to his throbbing cock before setting the bottle aside. There was no way he was going to risk hurting their Hannah. She was perfect for them when they'd thought a computer had picked out their perfect wife.

He lined up his cockhead with her tiny rosette and pressed forward, gently massaging her lower back as he fought to go slow. The feel of her tender tissues separating for him, sucking him in while trying to push him out was almost more than he could take. As she slowly relaxed around him so that he slid past the tight resistant ring of muscles, heat blossomed around his cock the deeper he forged. Her tightness was almost his undoing as she accepted him into her body. He would never forget this moment, this special instants when she trusted him in ways many would never offer. He could already feel love building for her in his heart.

"Hannah!" he called out as his pelvis met her ass cheeks.

"God, she's so tight. With you in her ass, I feel like I'm suffocating," Edward confessed from below.

"I'm never going to last. Help her, Edward." Porter felt as if his balls were already ready to explode. His voice sounded harsh even to his ears.

He felt Hannah squeeze around him, her moan telling him that Edward was playing with her, urging her toward her own completion. He furiously held on to his climax intent that she would come first.

"Fuck! So good," he hissed out as he powered in and out of her tight ass.

"Porter! Edward!" Hannah's husky voice called out just before she clenched around them, enclosing his dick in a tight fist of fire that threatened his very existence.

She screamed as she collapsed over Edward. Porter thrust into her once, twice, and then his orgasm consumed him. Fire shot from his spine to his balls and cum burned its way up his cock to fill her dark depths. He felt as if his toes had turned inside out. Nothing had ever felt that way before. He could have sworn that he could hear her thoughts there for a second. They had been so close, so a part of each other that he was sure he'd heard her heart beat his and Edward's name in his ear.

Chapter Seven

Hannah squirmed between Porter and Edward as they rode the short distance to Cam, Phillip, and Lacy's house. Oh, and she couldn't forget little Julie. She knew it was short for Julianne, and that she was nearly three.

Without knowing these people, just showing up out of the blue seemed awkward to her. What would they possibly have to talk about? Well, the guys had work to discuss, but Hannah didn't know Lacy. She prayed she didn't embarrass the guys by seeming rude when she didn't say much. She didn't want them to regret her being with them for even an instant, especially after last night. Last night had been—well, simply perfect.

"Relax, baby girl. It's going to be fine. You'll see. They seem like nice people and want to make sure we're prepared to handle everything. I'm sure you'll like Lacy just fine," Porter told her.

She squeezed his hand and nodded, forcing a broad smile across her face that she didn't really feel. She'd never been one to make instant friends.

"I don't really blame her for being nervous, Porter. This is a whole new life for us and she's been thrust into a relationship with two strange men and now she's going to meet a strange family as well. Got to be a little uncomfortable." Edward's support meant more to her than he'd ever know. He understood. He got how hard this was for her.

"I'm sorry, babe. We won't leave you alone if you don't feel comfortable with her," Porter assured her, squeezing her hand back.

"I'll be fine. I'm not a baby. I can handle a few hours of small talk." She did feel like a child now having allowed them to know how worried she was.

They pulled up outside a fence that surrounded a house much like theirs. Before Edward cut the engine to jump down and open the gate, a very tall man with a long brown ponytail hurried out to the gate carrying a gun. He made short work of unlocking it and letting them drive inside before shutting it behind them. Hannah had never seen a man as tall and broad shouldered as this man was. She actually shivered at the thought of having to stand anywhere close to him.

As soon as Edward had cut the engine, the big man had his door open and was reaching out to shake his hand.

"Great to have you guys over. I'm Cam. Come on inside," he said with a warm smile.

"I'm Edward. This is our wife, Hannah, and that's Porter," he said indicating them.

Cam grinned and nodded at them before stepping back for Edward to jump down. Porter helped her unfasten her harness then jumped down to help her out of the buggy. When they walked around to the porch, a lovely woman with long reddish-blonde hair stood next to another tall man with almost blue black hair who held a honey-blonde-haired child who looked much bigger than three years old.

"Welcome to our house. Come on in and let's eat. I hope you have a big appetite. Lacy went all out today. We're having a little of everything, I think," the other man said.

"That's Phillip and Lacy and our daughter, Julie," Cam pointed out as Porter led her up the steps to the porch.

"Great to meet you," Porter said holding out his hand to Phillip.

They greeted each other and entered the house where Cam set aside the large rifle and closed the door behind them. Lacy ushered them into the kitchen to where the table had the leaf added to make it much larger to accommodate all of them. It would probably hold twelve people if the need arose. She wondered if they had leafs for their table. As if reading her mind, Lacy answered her unasked question.

"The extra leafs are in the little slide out area in the pantry behind the door. I found them about six months ago by accident. I was trying to clean some peas up that Julie had spilled and got the broom stuck under the slide out door. I nearly screamed when they popped out of the wall," she said with a laugh.

"Had Cam jumping the couch to get to the kitchen to check on her," Phillip added with a chuckle.

"Mommy had da funniest wook on her fwace when Daddy Cam gwabbed her and picked her up," the little girl said.

Hannah and the guys stared at her with complete surprise. She sounded much too grown up for a three-year-old, especially one who wasn't really supposed to be three yet anyway.

"Um, Julie is very advanced for her age," Lacy said with a strained smile. "We'll talk more about that later."

Hannah took that to mean she didn't want to talk in front of Julie. Or maybe she just didn't want to talk about anything until after they'd eaten. For some odd reason, Hannah was more than happy to put that discussion off until later as well. She could feel the apprehension in the air so thick it was almost difficult to breathe around it.

"Something smells amazing," Porter said, breaking the tension for now. Hannah could have hugged him right then.

"Have a seat everyone. We don't have set places to sit here. Just wherever there's a chair," Cam said.

"We need to eat before it gets cold," Phillip added.

For the next hour, the conversation remained light and fun, punctuated with comments on how good everything tasted and questions on what some of it was. Hannah found herself relaxing around Lacy, asking about recipes. The woman promised that she'd already written everything up for her to take back then they left.

"I figured you could use some ideas other than the ones they probably taught you on the shuttle. We've been passing around information among us for about two years now and it saves us all a lot of time." Lacy reached over and poured more of the stone berry lemonade for Julie.

After everyone had eaten their fill, Hannah helped Lacy clean up and put everything away while the men retired to the office to talk business or farming or whatever they were going to discuss. She was fine while they cleaned and washed up, but once everything was done, Hannah began to feel a bit uncomfortable again. She still couldn't believe that no one had said one word about her name being Hannah and not Gladys. They would have known who was coming with Porter and Edward.

Then there was the fact that little Julie helped them put things away. She shouldn't be able to do much at her age, but the fact remained that she stood about the same height that she remembered her sister being at nearly four years old. Plus, she was so much more articulate for a nearly two-year-old.

"You don't have to worry, Mif Hannahy. Evewyting is good. Mommy and Daddy Cam and Daddy Phiwip wike you fine," Julie said patting her hand.

She had no idea how to answer that. Thankfully Lacy came to her rescue.

"Nap time, little lady," Lacy said with a smile.

"K, Mommy." Julie walked over to Hannah and pulled at her shirt until she bent over. The precious little girl hugged her tightly around the neck. "You awedy got a baby gwoing inside you. I heared his heart bweating."

With that whispered announcement, the precocious child followed her mommy out of the kitchen. Lacy called over her shoulder that she would be right back.

Hannah stood in the middle of the room still reeling from the little girl's claim. How could she already be pregnant? Yeah, she'd had unprotected sex like maybe five times now, but wasn't it too soon?

She was still standing in the same spot when Lacy walked back in the kitchen several minutes later.

"Are you okay?" she asked, obviously worried by her expression.

"Um, yeah."

"Whatever Julie told you, she didn't mean to upset you, but you need to know that she um, knows things sometimes." Lacy walked over to the fridge and pulled out the carafe of stone berry lemonade and grabbed two glasses before carrying them over to the table. "Have a seat and I'll tell you about some of the odd things that are happening here on Alpha."

Hannah found herself following the woman to the table. She lowered herself to a chair and waited as Lacy poured them more of the slightly tart drink. Once she'd taken a sip, Lacy began talking.

"You're going to find that children born on Alpha are different than those born on Earth were. They grow faster and mature quicker for one thing. A pregnancy doesn't last quite as long here either. Usually about seven months at the most."

"Why? I don't understand. I mean we're still regular people. One of us isn't an alien or anything," Hannah protested.

"That's true, but we are living, breathing, and eating from a planet we weren't born on. According to Doc Jeff at the space station, there are odd cells or enzymes or something in our blood now. We are probably getting them from the food we eat that is grown here and the water we drink. Even the beef we eat that we brought from Earth is feeding from the grass and grain we raised here."

"What is it going to do to us? Is it making us sick?" she finally asked.

Fear of the unknown set heavy in her belly after eating all of the food they had consumed earlier.

"No. It's not making us sick. If anything, it's making us stronger and healthier. We don't seem to get sick like we did on Earth. You know, colds and viruses. Some of us who've been bitten or scratched by some of the animals here have an added cell in our blood that seems to give us a higher resistance to everything," Lacy told her.

"How is Julie different other than the fact that she looks much older than nearly three?" Hannah finally asked.

Lacy wrapped her hands around her glass and stared down at it. It was obvious that she didn't want to share with her. Hannah guessed she couldn't blame the other woman. Talking about your child's oddities wasn't something you wanted to discuss with a virtual stranger you'd only just met.

"You need to know since you'll eventually have a child to raise. She's my precious child and I won't tolerate anyone upsetting her. Okay?" Lacy looked directly into Hannah's eyes with steel reserve.

"I would never hurt a child, Lacy. No matter what you say, she's still a child." Hannah tried not to feel resentful since Lacy didn't know her.

"The children here have special abilities. They aren't all the same ones either. One little boy can find people no matter where they are. You don't want to play hide and seek with him. It's impossible to hide from him." Lacy laughed. "Julie knows things about people. She can understand some of what they are thinking and we think she can understand some of the animals around here, too."

Hannah sat there quietly for a few seconds trying to digest what Lacy was claiming. If that were true, then it was possible she was already going to have a baby, but wasn't it too soon? How could she believe that an admittedly advanced child could know if she were already pregnant? It had been what, three days? Surely it wasn't possible to know that soon. Not even if the child could know things.

"Why do you think she can communicate with the animals?" she finally asked, unable to think of what to say.

"A muskie was sniffing around the fence one day when we were outside and she said it wanted in because it had left food buried in our yard. She worried about the muskie's food to the point that she was driving us crazy. Phillip finally asked her where it was so he could dig it up and throw it over the fence so she'd stop obsessing about it." Lacy sighed and shook her head. Hannah could tell the other woman was still getting used to her daughter's supposed abilities.

"She was able to show us exactly where each hidden catch of food was. Phillip and Cam dug it all up and tossed it over the fence. The muskie chattered at Julie then made several trips carting off its food. I'll never forget that as long as I live."

"I expect not. That's sort of scary," Hannah agreed. "Do you think the muskie would have hurt her if it had been able to get in?"

"You know, I never thought about it. I don't know." Lacy sipped her drink.

"Your daughter says I'm already pregnant. Do you think she's right? Do I believe her?" Hannah asked quietly.

Lacy smiled broadly. "Congratulations! If she says you are, then you are. That's wonderful!"

"So you believe her," Hannah said quietly.

"Absolutely, and you can, too."

"She called it a he, so I guess I need to be thinking of names for boys," Hannah almost whispered.

"Don't be scared, Hannah. Everything will be fine. You're not alone. There are three other families who live close by. We all take care of each other and help in any way we can. Elissa, Gray, and Clint live on the other side of us. They have a little boy, Mark, who's about ten months younger than Julie is. He's a sweet child, very quiet and calm. You'll meet them in a few weeks. We'll have a big gathering to celebrate the crops coming up." Lacy looked up when the men walked back into the kitchen.

"How are you two doing?" Cam asked while Phillip pulled the posco tea out to refill their glasses.

"Fine," they both said at the same time, then laughed.

The four men exchanged worried glances before joining them at the table. Hannah wasn't sure what would be said next. She didn't like the unease that hadn't left her since they'd left that morning to drive over. Her entire body felt sore from the sensation of being on guard for so long. She knew it was silly when they weren't in any danger from these people, but she still didn't feel as if she were a part of it all yet. Despite having become more comfortable, even feeling accepted by Edward and Porter, Hannah still harbored guilt over having assumed another identity and taking Gladys's place on board the shuttle.

"Lacy, we've talked to Edward and Porter about the children and everything. How is Hannah doing?" Phillip asked as he sat down next to his wife.

"I think she's handling it fine, aren't you?" Lacy asked looking across the table toward her.

"Um, I suppose. It's all a little overwhelming. I mean I knew things would be different from back on Earth, but this seems a little more than just different," she admitted.

"Believe me when I say we agree with you," Phillip said. "The thing is that we've got to adapt and keep building our home here. We can't worry over it overly much or we'll stagnate and end up failing to survive."

"Why are you so nervous around us, Hannah?" Cam asked all of a sudden.

Edward and Porter immediately took her hands in theirs and glared at the two men. She didn't want them to be at odds with the other family because of her insecurities. She squeezed their hands and looked at the other man.

"You haven't said anything about the fact that I'm not Gladys. I know you expected Edward and Porter to be married to her but you haven't said a thing about it. It makes me nervous that you're just waiting to spring it on me at some point," she admitted.

"You don't have to say anything, Hannah. It's none of their business," Porter said.

"He's right. It isn't our business. That's why we haven't said anything. When you arrived at the house and they radioed to introduce themselves, they told us that Gladys backed out of the deal and you agreed to take her place. That's all that matters. We're just glad you're here with them. End of story. Don't worry about it anymore. No one will question you're being here, Hannah," Cam assured her.

Oddly enough, a weight lifted from her shoulders at their assurance that they weren't concerned at all about her being there. It all seemed silly now and she realized she really had been making a big deal out of something that really didn't matter to anyone but her and the two men. If they had accepted her then why shouldn't everyone else? She sighed and relaxed back in the chair.

"Does everyone know about the children?" Edward asked. "I mean, it was never mentioned in all of the discussions we had on the shuttle."

"No. Only those of us with children know right now, but I think Doc Jeff is beginning to realize that there is something going on. We've been keeping it quiet from those back on Earth. You know how life was back there. They took over everything. Not that we're complaining about our lives here now, but we they didn't give some of us choices when they sent us here," Cam said.

"We were afraid they might try to take our children to study them," Phillip confessed.

"I can understand that. I wouldn't want them to know anything either. How are you going to keep it from them though? Someone is going to slip up before it's over with," Edward said.

"We just hope for the best. Plus, according to Doc Jeff and his wife who came over on your shuttle trip, Earth isn't going to hold together more than another three or four years. They're really scrambling to get people off the planet now," Phillip told them.

"I talked to their wife, Megan. She said that even though they've moved the women below ground, some of them are still getting Shear's disease anyway," Hannah told them.

"What are we going to do when they no longer bring supplies to us?" Lacy asked. "I mean, we still depend on so much from Earth."

"That's why we're trying to grow and create everything we can based on Alpha's resources. I thought all along that starting out with so much was just spoiling us to how things will eventually regress some after Earth is gone in a few years," Phillip told them.

"I think it was necessary to give us some comfort while we got started, Phil. If we'd have had to completely wing it from day one while trying to learn the dangers of the planet, we'd have never made it to begin with," Cam said.

Lacy chuckled. "Okay, guys. Let's not drag our guests into your debate." She looked at them. "If we let them, they'll argue for hours about it."

"As much as we'd like to stay and visit more," Porter began. "We need to get back before dark. I know we have an hour more here, but we still need to check the fence line and water the garden again."

"Oh! Right. I nearly forgot. How many rows did you plant?" Cam asked.

Hannah smiled and watched the two men exchange glances.

"Uh, why?" Edward asked.

Cam grinned. "Cause we have a bet going and I want to know if I won or not."

Edward smiled and shook his head. "Might as well tell them. They'll find out eventually anyway."

Porter grinned and shot Edward an obscene gesture. "We planted 25 rows."

"That were eight feet longer than your original plans," Hannah added with a mischievous grin. She ducked when Porter made as if to strangle her.

Lacy died out laughing as Phillip threw up his arms with disgust. Cam grinned and leaned over to kiss Lacy.

"I win," he said.

"What did you win?" Edward asked.

"Um, not going there, man." Phillip blurted out.

Everyone laughed at that as Lacy's face blossomed into a pretty pink color. Hannah knew without a doubt it centered on Lacy and sex for the other woman to have blushed like that. She stood up to draw the attention off of the other woman.

"We better go now. Tell Julie I said bye and thanks for the information," she said.

"What information?" Edward asked.

"I'll tell you later," she said with a smile. She wasn't sure what they would think about it and wanted a little time to let it sink in before she shared with them.

"Thank you for having us and for filling us in on what to expect," Porter told them.

"Here. Don't forget your recipes, Hannah." Lacy handed her a group of papers.

"Thanks again, Lacy. I might be calling you up on the radio in a few days to ask some more questions."

"Anytime. We're all in this together. Survival isn't a solitary activity. It's going to take us all working together to make it here."

Chapter Eight

Everyone had been quiet on the short trip back to their house. The sun still had a little while to go before it would sink below the horizon but Hannah was already ready to go to bed. Somehow, the entire day had taken a toll on her. She felt as if they'd planted the entire garden all over again.

"Since they were nice enough to send us home with leftovers, I vote we handle everything outside first and then eat an early dinner before heading to bed," Porter said.

"I agree," Edward said. "I'm tired. I guess I was a little tense about meeting with them after all."

"I'll get everything ready while you're outside," Hannah said. She carried one of the boxes of food in her arms as they walked inside the house.

Both men continued on through the back door back outside after dropping off their packages they'd carried in with them. Hannah sifted through everything and after selecting a couple of dishes, put away the rest for the next day. Then she set the table and returned to the living room to sit on the couch until they finished their chores outside. She had a lot to think about.

As she relaxed back on the couch, it occurred to her that the men might not be too happy to find out that she was already pregnant. It would put her having the baby right before winter. She would have to harvest and put up their vegetables when she was at her biggest. Hannah wasn't sure how well that was going to go over. She'd canned before but never alone and most certainly never while she was as big as a whale. At least while they were getting used to having a baby, the guys wouldn't be working as much with it being winter. Still, Hannah was a little worried about breaking the news to them.

As she lay back against the couch, it dawned on her that she couldn't share the news of her pregnancy with her sister and that her sister was back on a dying Earth with very little chance of surviving past another three or four years according to what the others had said. Tears pricked at the back of her eyes as she fought not to sink into depression. They'd talked about it before she'd left and Cathy had made Hannah promise she wouldn't make herself sick worrying about her all the time.

"Hannah, you've done more than you should have already. You're the best sister anyone could have every asked for. I love you. Now go and be happy. I love you and always will." Cathy had hugged her tightly before she'd left and shoved her backpack on her before she'd walked away.

Once she'd settled into her quarters, Hannah had opened her pack and found Cathy's stuffed cat from when she'd been a child and needed one to sleep at night. The note attached had said for her to give it to her first child from her Aunt Cathy. Hannah had barely managed not to fall apart over that and pushed it to the back of her mind until now. Neither of them would have believed that time would come some soon.

A little boy. If Julie could be believed, not only was she already carrying a child, it would be a boy. She wondered whose eyes he would have and what color his hair would be. She prayed he would be healthy and strong like his fathers. Then she worried about what sort of special talent he would have. How would they be able to help him deal with something like being able to read minds, or talk to animals or know things he shouldn't know?

She hadn't realized she'd even closed her eyes, much less fallen asleep until Porter was kissing her cheek and telling her it was time to eat. She rubbed her face and looked up to find both men grinning down at her.

"What?" she asked, more than a little confused.

"You have the cutest little snore," Edward said.

"I don't snore," she fussed, sitting up straight.

"Yes, you do, baby girl," Porter agreed.

She huffed at them before standing up and walking toward the kitchen. She wasn't about to start a discussion about whether she snored or not. She didn't snore. It would be two against one though so she had no way to win.

They ate the warmed-up remnants of lunch and talked about how good it was, even warmed up.

"I hope I can make some of these dishes even half as good as she did. To think that all of this is from their garden or the natural plants around the planet," she said.

"What you've fixed us so far has been delicious, honey. I wouldn't worry about following the recipes she gave you," Edward told her.

"Was everything okay outside? How does the garden look so far?" she asked.

"Everything is fine. We watered it but it still just looks like rows of dirt," Porter said with a chuckle. "Even if it does grow fast, it will still be another few days before we get any ground breakage."

"I can't wait to see it come up. I used to help put up from the garden, but I never actually planted anything before," she said. "It's going to be fun to watch it grow."

Porter laughed. "I always said watching the crops grow was a study in boredom, but maybe that will be different here on Alpha from what Cam and Phillip claim."

"What do you think about what Lacy told you about the children here, Hannah?" Edward asked, suddenly changing the subject.

She bit her lower lip and took a quick sip of the tea to clear her throat and give her another second of stalling. Finally she shrugged, not looking at them.

"It's all kind of hard to believe, but Julie is larger than she should be and can speak a lot better than I would expect at her age."

"Did she tell you about her ability to understand the animals on the planet?" Porter asked.

Hannah could feel their eyes on her. She finally nodded. "Yeah. It's kind of scary."

"She's able to know things, too, according to Phillip," Edward said.

"Um, yeah. Lacy said that, too." She drew in a deep breath and finally spit it out. She couldn't keep it from them. "She told me that I'm already pregnant. I'm having a little boy."

She heard a chair scrape against the floor then hit the ground. She jerked her head up in time to see Edward standing up at the end of the table with a look of horror on his face. Porter's expression held utter shock as well but at least he didn't look sick about it.

Hannah had been right. They weren't happy about it at all. She'd have been better off not telling them right away. Why hadn't she kept her mouth shut? Now everything would be different. They'd avoid her and worry about everything now. She jumped up and ran from the room. All she could think about was that everything had been going so well and now she'd ruined it.

She heard Porter calling after her, but Hannah ignored them and hurried up the stairs. She didn't want to talk to them again right then. As soon as she got to the bathroom, she closed the door and locked it. Then she turned on the shower and stripped out of her clothes. By the time she'd stepped into the spray, it had warmed to a tolerable temperature. It did nothing to comfort her or stop the tears that fell. Hannah sank to the tiled floor and hugged her knees to her as she sobbed softly under the sound of the water hitting the tile.

Why couldn't they have been happy to know that she was having their baby? Why did she have to get pregnant so soon in the first place? Everything had been going so well after they'd gotten past her deception. Now they were back at square one. How many times would they be able to forgive her before they couldn't any longer? What would happen when that time came? Hannah wished her sister was there once again. She felt so alone.

* * * *

"Damn! What in the hell just happened?" Porter asked, standing up to stare at Edward.

"She just told us she was pregnant. It's only been a few days! There's no way it can be ours that fast," he said, his face completely horrified.

Porter didn't even think, he just punched the other man in the face, watching him stagger back but not fall.

"What in the hell did you do that for?" Edward demanded.

"Are you fucking crazy? It only takes once to do the deed, man. You're old enough to realize that. I can't believe you said that! Of course it's our baby. She's been on a fucking shuttle just like us for the last six months." Porter just shook his head in disgust.

Edward sighed then rubbed his hands over his face. "You're right. I shouldn't have said that."

"Hell! You shouldn't have even thought it, man. What the fuck is your problem?" Porter demanded. "She's our wife regardless of whether we had a ceremony or not. That was Earth's tradition anyway. On Alpha we don't need a ceremony. The thing is that she's our woman and we just told her that we're not happy that she's having our baby. That's fucked up, man."

"You're right. I'm sorry. I panicked. Flashback to my fiancée eight years ago. I shouldn't have compared her to Lydia, but it hit me out of the blue man." Edward shook his head.

"I didn't even know you'd been engaged before. You never said anything before."

Edward shrugged. "It was a long time ago and in the past."

"Evidently it's not as much in the past as you thought. You reacted to Hannah based on it," Porter said shoving his hands in his pockets.

"I had been going out with this woman for a few months when she told me she was pregnant. I was devastated. I liked her, but I wasn't in love with her. I hadn't really gotten to the point of thinking seriously about her when she hit me with that. I was going to do the right thing, of course, and marry her. Got her an engagement ring and she planned the wedding while I tried to find a second job. I dropped out of college to do it."

Edward ran his hand over his face again. It was obvious that he'd buried this under a layer of skin for some time. He hadn't once mentioned that he'd ever been that close to getting married when they'd talked on the shuttle about their past.

He started talking again. "Then, about a month later I went with her to the doctor for her first appointment and when he did the ultrasound, he congratulated us and said she was about three months along. We'd only been having sex for about five weeks. She'd had sex with someone at least twelve weeks before. The thing about it was, we'd been dating for nearly five months but had only been intimate for about the last five weeks. She'd had sex with someone while we were together then tried to pass it off as my child."

"That's harsh, man. I'm sorry, but Hannah is not your ex. She's ours now and forever and she's having our baby. A little boy, Edward," Porter said, looking at the other man.

"What are we going to do, Porter? How can we possibly take care of Hannah, a baby, and be ready for winter when we don't know the first thing about this place? Hell, I thought we'd have a few months to figure things out before she got pregnant," Edward said in a raspy voice.

"Well, we don't. That's why Cam and Phillip wanted to meet us and tell us what to expect. They're there for us just like the other families are. We have to work together to make it here." Porter couldn't believe he was having this conversation with Edward.

The man had been like a rock the entire trip to Alpha when Porter had worried about everything. Now the shoe was on the other foot, and he wasn't sure he could be as convincing as Edward had been. His partner had the confidence that Porter had never carried before. Now it seemed that while Porter had always known he was going to be a farmer, Edward had been in college to start with, and farming had ended up being the result of a woman's deception. Was he going to let it continue to influence him? If he did, Hannah would be the one to suffer and Porter wasn't going to let that happen.

"Look, man. Hannah is a good woman. She doesn't deserve this. She's suffered enough already. She's probably thinking that we're angry with her for being pregnant already. I'm sure as hell not. I'm just surprised, but happy. You need to get your act together, before you talk to her again." Porter looked at the table, realizing that Hannah hadn't eaten much of anything. "Clean up before you come to bed and make damn sure you're straight with how you feel before you climb into that bed with her."

He stomped out of the kitchen to the foot of the stairs. Porter stood there with on hand on the rail for several seconds before finally climbing to the second floor to stand outside the bedroom. She wasn't in the bedroom but the bathroom door was closed and he could hear the shower going. As much as he wanted to join her, he knew she wouldn't welcome him right then. Instead he took off his boots and shirt then sat on the side of the bed and waited for her.

After several long minutes, he began to worry about her. She'd been upstairs for quite a while before he'd come up. The water was bound to be getting cold by now. Just as he started to stand up, the water shut off. It didn't take much for him to imagine her stepping from the shower with water running down her body as she reached for a towel.

He enjoyed patting her dry when they showered together. It would be even better when she was round with their child. He couldn't wait to kiss her belly and talk to their son. He'd tell them both how much he cared about them every day. She was giving them all a chance at a new life, a new beginning. He wouldn't let Edward's insecurities to ruin that. They all deserved a chance at happiness, a hope for a future they hadn't had back on Earth.

The bathroom door finally creaked open and Hannah stepped out, stopping when she saw him sitting there waiting on her.

Without looking up, she walked over to the dresser. "You're going to want to wait a few minutes. I used up all of the hot water. I didn't realize you'd be up so soon."

He watched as she pulled out an old cotton gown and underwear. It hit him again that she didn't have much with how she'd ended up on the shuttle. She deserved to have nice things to wear instead of the old things she'd brought with her.

Porter waited where he was as she dressed with her back to him. When she finally walked over to the bed to climb up, he stopped her.

"Wait, baby girl." Porter got up and walked around to where she stood poised to climb up.

"What?" Unease spread over her face.

Porter cupped her face between his hands and slowly lowered his head until his lips brushed softly against hers. He sipped at them, licking across the seam before nipping her lower lip. Then he kissed one corner before pulling back and looking into her pretty hazel eyes. He liked how the different shades of green and brown kept you guessing as to which color would be dominant at any given time of the day.

"Thank you, Hannah," he said.

"What?" Confusion replaced the unease he'd hated seeing.

"For giving us a son. For carrying our child inside of you and caring for it. I promise we will protect you and him with our lives."

"You weren't so happy a little while ago. Hell, Edward was horrified. Don't say something you don't really mean, Porter. I get that it's too soon, there are too many things that we need to get done first, but I can't help it." Her voice broke but she didn't start crying.

"Shh, baby. I was surprised, but not the least bit upset about it. You have to admit that it's pretty damn shocking to know we're going to be having a little baby boy after only knowing each other for a few days. That just doesn't happen, or at least it didn't happen on Earth. Here on Alpha, well, I guess with children like Julie there's no need to wait for tests or ultrasounds to know when it's going to happen." He couldn't stop the grin that took over his mouth.

"You're really okay with it?" she asked, her eyes flicking upward to meet his before dropping once again. He hated that they'd lost the easy way they'd had between them only that morning.

"I'm really okay with it. I'm excited and scared, but happy. Everything will be fine, Hannah. Look at me, baby girl." He lifted her chin until she had no choice but to look at him. "He's going to be healthy and amazing."

"I'm scared, Porter. The children here are so different. How can we take care of them when they're different from us? Lacy said I'll only carry him for about six or seven months at the most." She gnawed at her lower lip.

Porter brushed his finger over where she was chewing on her lip to make her stop. Then he kissed her forehead.

"Don't worry about that yet. Let's get you past the morning sickness stage first. Get in bed and cover up. I'm going to take quick shower. I'll be back in a few minutes and we'll cuddle and talk about it." He helped her up on the bed then covered her with the sheet. "I won't be long."

"Porter?" she called out to him.

"Yeah?"

"Edward's not okay with this, is he?" she asked.

"He's okay, Hannah. It surprised him is all. He needs to talk to you about why he got so upset, but it wasn't because of you. He'll be up as soon as he finishes cleaning up downstairs."

At least Porter hoped he would. If the foolish idiot slept downstairs on the couch, he'd kick the man's ass.

"I'll be right back." Porter squeezed her hand then walked into the bathroom to shower so he could climb into bed with his woman as soon as possible.

* * * *

Once the last dish was dried and put away, Edward sighed and spread the dishcloth over the edge of the sink before turning and leaning against the cabinet. He'd washed the dishes by hand instead of just putting them in the dishwasher because he needed the time to think. He'd fucked up—again. Why was he always doing that around Hannah?

All he could think when she'd said she was pregnant was that there hadn't been enough time for her to know that. She had to have been with someone else like Lydia had to already know she was having a baby. Hell, she'd even said it was going to be a boy. He never even considered that Julie would know and tell her something like that. No, all Edward had thought about was that she had a nice round tummy he like to rub and kiss and she was telling them that she was going to have a baby.

He groaned and hung his head. She would never forgive him for this. He had no doubt that he'd looked horrified as he'd jumped up and knocked the chair over behind him. Why had he reacted like that?

Because I still blame Lydia for the fact that I'm a farmer and not the stockbroker I'd planned on being.

Then he laughed. Actually, Lydia had probably saved his life. If he'd become a stockbroker like he'd planned on becoming, he wouldn't have had the skills needed to be chosen to come to Alpha.

Who knew back then that being a lowly farmer like his dad and his granddad would be so important to him one day? He'd studied hard, strived to make it to the top of his class so he would get the scholarships it would take to go to a premier university so he could climb out of the farming family he'd been born into.

Then Lydia had come along and ruined it all for him. By the time he'd realized that the baby couldn't be his, he had lost his scholarships and the chance to better himself. His dreams were all gone and he was right back where he'd started, a farmer. Yeah, he'd gone off the deep end for a few weeks, drinking and wallowing in misery like any normal eighteen-year-old might have done, but he'd picked himself up and accepted that it just wasn't going to happen. He'd screwed up letting his dick control him. He never should have slept with Lydia in the first place. Then there would never have been any doubt that the child hadn't been his.

While he'd resented losing out on the opportunity to go on to college and make something of himself after all of the hard work he'd put into it, Edward had accepted his circumstances and poured himself into farming to be the best he could be. It had paid off when their land produced the most and best vegetables every year. Because of that, he and his brother had been chosen as suitable candidates for one of the new planets.

They had chosen not to be paired up, knowing how competitive they tended to be. It would have been a disaster trying to share a wife between them. Andrew had left three months earlier than he had for Omega. He hoped he was happy wherever he was and doing a hell of a lot better than Edward was at that moment.

For a brief moment, he thought about sleeping on the couch until he could figure out how to tell Hannah how sorry he was about the way he'd reacted. He had to admit that it would only make things worse if he didn't go on up and admit his stupidity right away. He'd already put it off longer than he should have. He should have gone right up there and begged her to forgive him instead of hiding in the kitchen like a coward. Edward had never been a coward, but with the realization that they were about to start a family on a strange planet with even stranger animals where their children wouldn't exactly be normal, feeling a little cowardly didn't seem all that embarrassing.

He pushed away from the cabinet and walked straight through the living room to the stairs and climbed them without stopping. He did hesitate outside their bedroom door for a second, but forged ahead and pushed open the door to find Hannah sitting on the side of the bed with Porter next to her rubbing her back. She had on the most hideous nightgown he'd ever seen with red swollen eyes that refused to meet his when he walked into the room.

Without saying a word, Edward dropped to his knees in front of her and took her hands in his.

"I'm sorry, Hannah. I'm so, so sorry for how I reacted. It had nothing to do with you and everything to do with me. I'm happy about the baby, honey. I was reacting because of something that happened in my past but that's no excuse. Can you forgive me?" he asked, kissing the cool fingers he held in his hands.

She didn't look up at him. "It's okay, Edward. I know you weren't wanting to start a family so soon. We don't know anything about what to expect."

"No. It's not okay, honey. I let something that happened to me a long time ago bleed all over you and that's not right or fair to you. I'm so sorry." He felt Porter's hand touch his shoulder and looked up to see him shaking his head.

His friend obviously didn't think it was a good idea to tell her exactly what he'd been thinking when he'd reacted like he had. Maybe he was right, but he didn't like keeping it from her either.

"I promise, I'm very happy that you're carrying our child. I was surprised and after talking with Cam and Phillip about what all to expect here, I panicked. I'm sorry, Hannah. Please forgive me."

She finally looked up at him for a brief moment before nodding and dropping her head again. "It's okay, Edward. There's nothing to forgive."

He wrapped his arms around her waist and buried his head in her lap. The realization that life bloomed inside of her finally hit him and he buried his face against her belly. Then he was pulling at the ugly gown to get it off of her.

"What are you doing? Edward?" Hannah struggled to keep the gown in place but he was determined to get it off of her.

"I want to touch you, honey," he said. Thankfully Porter was on board with the idea of getting her naked.

"I don't want to sleep naked anymore," she said in a tear-tinged voice.

Edward didn't even bother to answer her. Instead he laid his cheek against her abdomen and rubbed there as they laid her back on the mattress. He turned and kissed her soft round tummy and was thankful that she wasn't fighting them any longer.

Chapter Nine

Hannah didn't know what to think anymore. Too much had happened in the last few days. She'd had to get past Edward's anger that she'd shown up instead of Gladys, then she'd found out that not only was she pregnant but her child wouldn't be just like them. Then Edward had flipped out on her again. She didn't think she could handle much more. Everything she knew was back on a dying Earth. Her sister, destined to die among strangers who Hannah had no idea if she could really trust them to take care of her or not had always been the positive one. She'd always believed that things would work out. Hannah hadn't. She'd grown up enough before things went to hell to know how cruel people could be. Her sister was only just finding that out.

The feel of Edward's lips on her belly had the tears falling all over again. She felt so alone. Even Porter wasn't enough to make her feel loved and cared for. They were stuck with her and had they been given a choice, she was sure they never would have picked her. Knowing that she was only a conciliation prize hurt far more than she would have believed at this point in her life. Hannah had thought she was past that. Evidently she wasn't.

"Please forgive me, Hannah. I really am happy that you're carrying our baby," Edward told her again.

"I–I said there wasn't anything to forgive. Stop, Edward." She tried to push him off of her, but he wouldn't budge.

He had wrapped his arms around her waist and was resting his cheek against her belly. Porter was lying next to her with his face buried against her neck. She didn't know what to do, what to say. She just wanted to forget it and go to sleep. Sleep would be really good right then.

Finally he pulled back and looked up at her. She could have sworn there were tears in his eyes, but she decided it was just a trick of the light from the two moons shining through the windows.

"I'm going to take a shower. I'll be right back, okay?" He seemed to be asking for her permission.

"I'm not going anywhere, Edward."

He stared into her eyes for a few long seconds then nodded and backed off the bed. When he was gone Porter pulled the covers up over them and spooned her from behind.

"He's scared you're going to reject him, Hannah. If you want to make him crawl for a little longer, I don't blame you, but he really is sorry for how he acted," Porter told her.

"I can't really blame him. I showed up instead of the woman he married. I'm nothing like someone he would have chosen, either of you really. I'm not all that pretty and I'm overweight, and now I'm going to have a baby that none of us was ready for. I can't seem to do anything right." She didn't have any more tears to cry now.

"Oh, baby. That's not true. You're perfect for us. You have the prettiest eyes that sparkle when you're happy. I love how your hair shines in the sun when we're outside. I love how soft your skin feels when I touch it. I don't like stick figure women with bones that stick out." He kissed her shoulder. "I'm crazy about you, baby girl."

Hannah wanted to believe him, wanted to trust that he wasn't just trying to make her feel better. She was just like any woman. She wanted to believe that she was the most important person in her man's life. In her case, she had two men to please. If just one of them really cared about her like that, she'd be happy, but she was afraid to believe. It would kill her to find out later that it had all been a lie.

She heard the water shut off in the bathroom. Edward would be back soon. She had hoped to be asleep before he got back into bed.

Somehow the thought of facing him again was more than she could handle.

Just as he opened the bathroom door, Hannah turned over in the bed and buried her face in her pillow so she wouldn't have to see his expression. She was sure it would be resignation.

"Hannah?" His voice sounded so unsure.

"Night, Edward," she said.

He climbed into bed and scooted up close to her, wrapping one hand over her hip. His hand was so warm, felt so good there. Hannah wanted to believe he cared so badly that it hurt.

"Night, honey." He kissed her shoulder then the light on the table next to the bed went out and he squeezed her hip.

She squeezed her eyes shut and prayed that sleep would come fast. She wasn't so lucky though. Long after the men were sleeping, Hannah lay awake trying to remain still and quiet. There wasn't a sound in the house as far as she could hear. No normal creaking of an old house since this one was so new and no humming electrical sounds interrupted the endless silence between the guys' soft snores.

She missed the constant noise that had surrounded her when she'd lived with the others in the bunkers. Not because it had been comforting but because it had meant that she was still with her sister and a few people that she thought were her friends. Here, she didn't know what to believe. Did she just go on as if nothing was wrong? How long could she live like that? How long before the constant strain of feeling like an imposter in what was supposed to be her home and her family tore her apart?

Hannah stifled a sigh. She didn't want to wake them up. They'd try and tell her everything was fine again. It wasn't and nothing would change that. She had to come to terms with it and figure out how to live with it. If it had been just her, Hannah would have asked them to take her back to the space station and figure out somewhere to work. She couldn't do that now, though. She had a child to think about and whether they were ready for him or not, the baby was their son.

She ran her hand over her pelvis and wondered if he was aware enough yet to feel her? She had to accept him and make sure he never felt as if he wasn't wanted like she did. She loved him even if he would be different, more than her. She would make sure her son never knew the fear of being alone. Whatever his differences were, she'd make sure he saw them as special, something to be proud of. With the other children having the same differences, he'd be accepted.

It was her last thought as sleep finally pulled her under. Even in sleep though, her dreams kept at her, reminding her that she wasn't really wanted, but she'd be sure her son was.

* * * *

When Hannah woke the next morning, neither man was in bed with her. She glanced over at the clock on the bedside table and realized it was nearly nine in the morning. She'd overslept. At least she hadn't had to face the men first thing. With that happy thought, she climbed out of bed and quickly made it before finishing up in the bathroom and dressing.

When she walked downstairs, she could hear the men in the kitchen. The fact that they'd had to make their own breakfast had her feeling like a failure once again. She shook it off and stepped into the room.

"Hey, baby girl. We'd hoped you would sleep a little longer. Did we make too much noise?" Porter asked walking toward her.

"No. I just woke up. I'm sorry I overslept. Did you get enough to eat? I can make something else," she said.

Porter stopped in front of her and pulled her into his arms. "We're fine. What would you like to eat? We've got left over breakfast meat of some kind and toast."

She wrinkled her nose at the thought of what they might have fixed. Some of the things they had here on Alpha had to be cooked a certain way or it wasn't really that tasty. She pulled back and gave him a smile.

"I'm not really very hungry right now. I'm going to have a piece of toast and some juice. It will be lunchtime soon anyway," she said turning toward the refrigerator.

"You sit down, honey. I'll get you something to drink." Edward grabbed her around the waist and hauled her back against him.

When he picked her up and carried her to the table, she had to bite her tongue to keep from demanding that he put her down. Instead, she forced herself to relax as he settled her in a chair at the table where Porter was setting up toast and some kind of jelly or jam for her to choose from.

"Thanks." She didn't look up at him.

"Do you want the stone berry or that orange stuff?" Edward asked her.

"Um, the orange stuff. I think it's called Gatorade, like back on Earth," she said.

"You're kidding. It doesn't taste anything like Gatorade," he said setting it on the table in front of her.

"Yeah, I didn't think so either. Maybe a little like Tang used to, but not much." Porter poured some of it in a glass for her.

"Thanks. I'm good. You can go do whatever it is you need to be doing," she said, picking up a spoon to dip out some of the jelly to spread on the toast.

"We don't have anything we need to be doing except maybe you," Porter told her.

When she looked up at his comment it was to find him wiggling his eyebrows at her. She knew she was blushing from how hot her cheeks grew. How could they think about sex with everything that was going on?

Oh, right. I'm talking about men. They always think about sex.

"When do you start working?" she asked, ignoring his blatant suggestion.

"We don't start till day after tomorrow. We need time to get acclimated and settle in here first. How are you feeling this morning?" Edward asked looking down at her belly.

She refused to burst into tears. What was wrong with her? She wasn't far enough along to be this emotional.

"I'm fine. No nausea or anything for you to worry about." She bit off a portion of the jelly-covered bread.

"We thought we would make a trip back to the space station to load up on some things we're probably going to need. With us going to work soon, there won't be much time to make a trip later," Porter told her.

"Okay. I need a few things if you don't mind getting them for me while you're gone. I'll make a list," she said standing up.

"Hey, where are you going?" Edward asked, pushing her back on the chair. "Finish your breakfast. We've got plenty of time."

"And we're not going anywhere without you, baby girl. There's no need for you to make a list for us," Porter told her with a frown.

"Couldn't I just stay here while you go? I'm sure you don't need me hanging around while you take care of things," she said without looking up.

"The main reason we're going is to take you, honey. We wanted to get some things for you," Edward said sitting down next to her.

"What kind of things? I don't need anything, guys." She frowned across to where Porter stood next to the fridge.

"You don't have very many clothes, baby girl. And you need to see the doctor to get vitamins for the baby," he said.

"Oh. I guess you're right about the vitamins, but I don't need many clothes, guys. I'm just going to outgrow them anyway," she said looking back down at her plate and losing her appetite at the thought of gaining more weight.

"I can't wait to see you get a basketball belly," Porter teased with a huge grin.

"It's not funny, Porter. I'm already big enough as it is. I'm going to get huge." Hannah ran her hands over her face and sat back in the chair, no longer the least bit hungry.

"Stop it right now, Hannah," Edward said, his voice had gotten deeper and he'd turned in his chair to stare at her. "You're not too big at all. You're perfect. We want you healthy and the baby healthy. That means you're going to get all round and soft with our baby. There's nothing wrong with that."

"You say that now, but once the baby comes, I'll still be fat and it won't be easy getting the weight off." She was just like her mom and she'd always had to fight to keep from getting too big.

"I promise, honey. No matter how big you get, Porter and I will enjoy helping you work it back off. You won't be able to go two steps without one of us trying to help you exercise," Edward told her.

She just shook her head. They had no idea. She knew what it would be like. The baby would need tending and all of them would be too tired to do more than take care of the baby and work and keep the house. No, she wasn't going to candy coat or romanticize pregnancy or afterward. She'd watched her parents and her friends with their children. Parenthood was a major event that never turned off.

"Eat up, sweet thing. We're going to have fun today. You'll see," Porter said gesturing at her plate.

"I'm finished. I'll grab something to take with us as a snack in case I get hungry later." She stood up, picking up her plate to carry it to the sink.

"I've got that." Edward took it away from her then picked up her empty glass as well. "Do you want more juice before I wash this?"

"No thanks." Hannah wasn't sure how to act around the two men. They were pretending that everything was fine yet still seemed uncomfortable around her.

Twenty minutes later, Edward strapped her into the transport as Porter got them ready to head out. She wasn't sure why they wanted to take her with them, but she wasn't going to argue. Getting out would be good when she was sure it would be a while before she'd get to go back.

The drive over didn't seem to take as long as she had remembered it taking out there, but then it was full daylight and they weren't anxious about where they were going to live. While they didn't see any of the strange and scary mantises they did catch sight of some dorries watching as they passed.

The first place they went on arriving was the clinic. Before they got out of the transport she reminded them not to say anything about Julie's part in her knowing she was pregnant. She was just going to admit to having some breast soreness and nausea. She would tell the doctor that she just *knew* she was pregnant and chalk it up to a woman's intuition.

They assured her they weren't going to say anything though they both thought it wasn't a good idea to keep something like that from their only doctor. She just knew it wasn't her secret yet to reveal.

When they arrived, it was to find Scott, the doctor's nurse, the only one there at the moment.

"The doctor had to go check on a patient. He'll be back later if you want to come back," he said.

"No, there's no need really. I just need to get some vitamins. I'm pregnant and figured that I should get started on them as soon as possible."

"We can come back later," Edward said with a frown.

"Really. There's no need yet. When I'm farther along, he'll want to check me then, but right now, I just need the pills." She stared hard at him, willing him to understand that she didn't want to have to lie to the man.

"Well, congratulations! That's wonderful to hear. You just arrived, didn't you?" he asked, watching her closely.

"Our wife is a fertile woman," Porter said, hugging her close. "She's made us so happy."

"Well, while you're here, I'll go ahead and draw your blood and get you set up on prenatal vitamins. What symptoms are you having?" he asked.

"Um, well, my, um, breasts are tender and I've been a little sick to my stomach the last two mornings," she said without looking at him.

"And you're sure you're already pregnant," he said as he ushered them into a room.

"Yes. I just know. I don't know how to explain it," she said, honestly not knowing what she could say to convince him.

"Oh, I'm sure you do. Women tend to know these things," he said with a chuckle. He turned to the men. "Help her up on the table and I'll get my supplies."

It was Edward who swung her up on the table as if she weighed nothing. He didn't move away from her though. Instead, he wrapped an arm around her waist, pulling her close to him as Porter held her hand on the other side. She wasn't sure if it was all for show of if they were just trying to convince her that they were serious about being happy about the baby.

"Okay. I'm going to check your blood pressure and temperature and then draw your blood," Scott said as he wrapped a cuff around her upper arm.

Twenty minutes later, they were waiting in the hall that seemed to serve as a waiting room while they waited for Scott to label and put away the blood before giving them the vitamins. After several minutes, he returned with a small bag.

"Here you go. There is two months' worth in the bag plus two months of iron tablets. Even with the prenatals, the women here tend to stay fairly anemic so go ahead and take them until you come back in to see the doc. You should probably plan to see him in the next forty-five or so days for a thorough checkup. If he finds anything unusual in the blood results, he'll call you up on the radio." Scott shook the men's hands and congratulated them all.

"Oh, I nearly forgot to ask. How is Megan doing? I met her on the shuttle. We were in the same area." Hannah was ashamed that she hadn't said anything before now.

"She's fine. Settling in well here. Thanks for asking. I'll tell her you asked about her."

"See you in a few weeks, Scott." Edward took the bag from Hannah's hand and waved at the other man as they walked toward the door.

Once outside, the men steered her toward a row of stores several doors down from the clinic. She felt like that had gone well enough, although she had hoped that if she was going to have to come to the space station she might at least get to talk to Megan. She hadn't really gotten to know any of the other women very well. For some reason Megan had befriended her almost from the start.

"Here we go. This one looks like it should have what you need to tide you over for a few weeks," Porter said, opening the door to one of the shops.

When she stepped into the building Hannah nearly turned and ran. It held nothing but underwear as far as she could tell, and not normal underwear either, fancy, lacy things. She could already feel her face warming at the sight of the sheer underthings hanging around.

"Hi there. What can I help you with?" The pretty woman who came forward to help them was probably about Hannah's age yet she seemed so much older with how she carried herself.

"Um, I'm not sure…" she began only to have Edward cut her off.

"We're looking for some pretty things for our wife." He smiled down at her and winked.

Porter had wondered off but quickly returned with a matching pair of pale pink panties and the demi bra that was attached to them. While pretty, she just couldn't see herself wearing them. She'd feel stupid with something like that under jeans and a T-shirt while she was out weeding the garden.

"I don't think this is a good place for me to shop, Edward," she whispered.

"Of course it is, honey. You'll look gorgeous in pink. I can't wait to see it on you," he said.

"They probably don't have any to fit me, Edward. Can we go? Please?" she almost begged.

He frowned. Then looked over at Porter and pointed to the door. Porter nodded but continued looking at the selections the pretty woman was showing him. Hannah wanted to cry but couldn't blame Porter for staying there. She followed Edward out the door and kept walking until he stopped her.

"Hey, where are you going?" he asked.

"Back to the transport to wait until you're ready to go." She tried to pull her hand from his, but he didn't let go.

"No. You're not going to sit in the transport and wait like an errant child. Why didn't you think they would have your size in there, Hannah? I'm sure they do. I bet Porter comes out with several things for you. I wanted to see you try on some of them," he said.

"Edward, I'm not that small. They don't make clothes like that to fit someone like me." She was horrified that he'd even suggest that she could wear any of those things. She'd hang over if she even managed to get them on in the first place.

"We've got to get something straight right now, Hannah. You're not fat. You're curvy in all the right places. Of course they have clothes to fit you," he said with an even deeper frown. "I don't understand where you got the idea that you're so big? We've never thought of you as big."

"Because back on Earth, they could never get clothes to fit some of us. We always ended up with men's shirts and jeans. The women who handed out supplies and clothes were always complaining about those of us who were so hard to fit. They kept saying it was a good thing we were fertile or we'd be out on the streets with the rest of them because we were too big to fool with." Hannah had to swallow hard to keep from crying. It shouldn't still hurt, but it did.

"Honey. You're not big. They were just jealous because you had curves they didn't have. I can't believe they let anyone talk to you like that. You're perfect, Hannah. Stop putting yourself down." Edward pulled her into his arms then lowered his mouth to hers to kiss her.

Hannah felt the pressure of his lips as he urged her to open for him. When he licked along the seam, she finally let him in and moaned at the wonderful taste of him as he explored her mouth, running his tongue along hers before sucking on it. When he finally pulled back, Hannah wasn't sure which way was up. They'd kissed her before, but not nearly as thorough as Edward just had.

"No more nonsense about being too big or anything. I mean it, Hannah. I hear you put yourself down once more and I'm going to turn you over my knee and spank that delicious ass of yours. Understand?" he asked, looking into her eyes.

All she could do was nod as he clasped her fingers with his and pulled her alongside him toward the next store. By the time they'd looked around at the shoes and boots, Porter had rejoined them with a giant smile on his face.

"I can't wait for you to try on what I picked out. You're going to look amazing in them," he said.

Hannah's mouth flew open in horror. "You bought me underwear in there?"

He grinned. "I sure did. They're all wrapped up in the transport."

She started to say something but Edward cleared his throat and she remembered his promise to spank her if she said anything bad about herself. Since she didn't know what he'd consider bad, she kept her mouth shut.

"Did you find some boots yet? You're going to need them once it gets cold." Porter pulled her toward the shoes once again.

For the next thirty minutes, they had her try on boots and shoes until she finally confessed to being hungry. Still, they ended up getting a pair of boots and a pair of shoes that would be more comfortable for working in the garden.

"The store clerk said there's a sandwich shop down here somewhere," Porter told them.

They found it nestled near a coffee shop. Hannah really was starving now. She hadn't eaten much the night before and only once slice of toast that morning. It was past noon now. When they ordered, she opted for a salad and a bowl of soup, but both men vetoed that and told her she could have either the salad or the soup but with a sandwich of some type.

"You've got to keep up your strength, honey. You're carrying a child that's going to be growing very fast. Remember?" Edward said.

"That soup and salad wouldn't last you two hours, baby girl. You need something more substantial in you," Porter added.

With a sigh, she knew they were right. She couldn't try and keep her weight down while she was pregnant. It wasn't the time. She would have to worry about it once she'd had the baby. Then she would worry about how to work on having a better figure so they would be happy. No matter how much they protested that they liked her just like she was, Hannah knew how men thought. They'd told her often enough when she was a teenager.

She prayed that she wouldn't gain too much weight with the baby. If she got as big as a house, she'd have so much more trouble than if she only gained ten or fifteen pounds. With the men stuck with her like they were, having an affair wasn't quite the option it had been on Earth, but knowing they didn't desire her or were disgusted by her would kill her.

"I can't wait to see you try on some of those clothes in the store next door. Are you finished, Hannah?" Edward stood up and held out his hand.

She'd hoped they would bypass that one. She'd seen some of the tops and dresses inside through the window. She didn't want to have to tell them something didn't fit over and over again, but maybe if she did, they'd realize she was right and stop pushing her to try on something she knew she'd look like a beached whale in. With that happy thought, Hannah followed them out of the café and into the women's shop. A tiny woman of about twenty-five met them just inside the door.

"Oh, look at you. I'm going to have so much fun fitting you!" she gushed and grabbed Hannah's hand to pull her toward the back of the store.

Chapter Ten

"Don't worry about anything. You two just have a seat over there and I'll bring her out to let you see what she looks like so you can choose your favorites," the woman said.

Hannah wasn't sure what to think as the woman shoved her into a dressing room and told her to strip. She stood in her underwear, arms crossed waiting for the lady to return with God knew what sort of clothes. She expected that none of them would fit and she'd be so embarrassed when she couldn't model anything for the men.

"Here we are." The sales clerk pushed into the dressing room with an arm load of clothes and set about hanging them on the hooks around the space. "My name is Anna and one of my husbands and I run this store and the other one helps manage the space station. What do your men do?"

Before she could answer, the woman was handing her something to put on. She looked at it and cringed. It was a dress. She never looked good in dresses. Plus, why would she need one here when they were just trying to survive? Still, she wasn't going to be rude when the woman had been nice so far.

"They are farmers," she said as she pulled the pretty sage material over her head, praying it would at least fit.

"Ooh! They're so important to all of us. We have to have the food they grow to live. Even if they are only growing the grain or the hay for the cattle, we wouldn't have meat without them. I sure don't want to eat any of those mantis creatures they talk about." She shivered daintily then giggled. "Now, turn around and let me zip you up. I do believe it fits perfectly!"

Sure enough, when Anna zipped the dress, it fit without pulling or cutting off her air. She turned to look in the full length mirror in the dressing room and was surprised by what she saw. In the mirror stood a woman wearing a pretty sage green dress that seemed to have been made to fit her slightly rounded belly and gently swelled hips. It didn't look like a sack stretched over her or a tent meant to hide her. She looked up with tears in her eyes to see Anna frowning at her in the mirror.

"Is something wrong?" the other woman asked.

"No. Not at all. Thank you. This is so pretty."

The woman smiled but still looked a bit worried. "Go show your men while I decide what you should try on next. That is absolutely amazing on you."

For the next hour, Hannah let Anna dress her in everything from dresses to shorts, trusting the woman to steer her in the right direction. Over and over again Anna talked about how much she wished she had Hannah's curves.

"Next to you, I feel like a bean pole. I can't wait until I start showing and put on some weight in a few months," she said.

"Showing? Are you pregnant?" Hannah asked.

"Yes. Just a few weeks, but I'm so excited!" Anna exclaimed.

"So am I! We're going to be having our babies about the same time, I bet." Hannah laughed, excited at the prospect of someone to talk to who seemed to like her.

"Oh, my God! That's wonderful! I'm six weeks. How far along are you?" she asked.

Hannah wasn't sure what to say. "I'm not exactly sure yet. I'm not seeing the doctor until another day. He was out seeing patients today when we came in. I got vitamins though so that I'll be healthy."

"You have to come back when you're ready for maternity clothes. We've got the best ones you could imagine. Some of them would be perfect with your hair and skin color. This is wonderful!"

They continued chatting as they left the dressing room for the last time. Porter and Edward looked perfectly content sitting on the chairs talking when she walked out. They both jumped up when they saw her walking toward them.

"Is that all? We were enjoying watching you try things on," Edward said.

"I think I've tried on everything they have in the store. I'm about worn out. Anna's been great!"

"We can't thank you enough for taking care of our wife for us," Porter said.

"It was my pleasure! She's the sweetest person! So, what did you pick out?" Anna asked walking with them over to the rack of clothes by the counter.

Hannah had to veto some of the outfits as not being practical enough for living on a farm but did let them get her two dresses to wear for special occasions.

"It's not a good idea to buy too much when I'm going to change in a few months. I might not ever be able to fit into these clothes again after the baby." Before Edward could say anything with the scowl that settled over his face, she pushed on. "When you have a baby, your body changes, guys. I might have larger boobs and that means some of those things won't fit anymore."

That got their attention and smoothed over Edward's obvious annoyance at her comment about not fitting into her clothes after the baby. Both men eyed her chest with obvious appreciation and perhaps some anticipation as well. She didn't bother smothering the giggle that escaped.

"Why don't you stay here until we get this all loaded into the transport, baby girl?" Porter kissed her then grabbed two bags while Edward managed three. "We'll be right back to get you."

"I can come with you," she said.

"No need. We've got one more store to look at down this way before we leave. You'd just be making an extra trip for nothing. Rest.

You're bound to be tired after trying on all of those things. We'll be right back," Edward assured her before slipping out the door.

"They love you very much," Anna said with a broad smile.

Hannah started. "Oh, well, I think it's too soon for that. We don't really know each other very well yet."

"Sometimes all it takes is a look. I think they took one look at you and fell head over heels for you. It's so obvious how happy they are with you."

"Maybe," was all she said.

Anna got busy with another customer, leaving Hannah to stew on the other woman's words. She hoped that they did care about her for more than the fact that she was having their baby, but she didn't think it was love. It was too soon.

But I already feel as if I love them. I want more than anything to make them happy and for them to love me back.

She could only pray that time would bind them closer to her until they did fall in love with her. She wanted that so very much.

After several more minutes of waiting, Edward walked in and strode directly to her. "Ready, honey?" he asked.

"Where is Porter?" she asked.

"He's waiting for us next door." He led her toward the front of the store and Hannah waved bye to Anna.

When they walked into the store, Hannah couldn't understand why they would be in a store that had jewelry and pictures and such in it. She wasn't one to want to decorate her home with all that sort of stuff. She hoped they didn't want to live in a fancy home.

"Why are we here?" she asked Edward in a soft voice.

"You'll see. Come on." He drew her with him toward where Porter stood talking to a man behind a counter filled with pretty jewelry.

She dragged her feet as they drew closer to where Porter was studying something on top of the glass case. When she stood just behind him, Edward spoke up.

"Did you find something?"

Porter turned and grinned like a child at Christmas. "I sure did. Come here, Hannah."

She took a step closer and Edward pushed her the rest of the way. "What are you doing?" she asked.

"You don't have a ring, baby girl. You need a ring." Porter picked up one and held his other hand out for hers.

"I don't have to have a ring, guys." She was mortified. If they'd been married back on Earth she would have had one already.

"We want one that we picked out on your finger, honey," Edward said and pushed her closer to Porter.

When Porter took her hand and slid the ring on her finger, she was sure it wouldn't fit, but it did—perfectly. She dragged her eyes from Porter's to look down at her hand and gasped. It was perfect. How had he known what she would like?

The sliver ring had no stones, but was etched with black Celtic designs that called to her. She hadn't wanted a gold band or one with diamonds in it. Porter had picked out the perfect ring. There was no way she could refuse it. She just nodded and looked up to see him grin even wider.

"Told you she'd like this one," he said as he bent down and kissed it on her finger.

"My turn," Edward said and pulled her to him for a proper kiss. When he let her go, she felt light headed and would have dropped to the ground if he'd let her go.

"Looks like you decided on the little love knot," the man behind the counter said. "Great choice."

"Thank you for all of your help," Edward told the man. "Are you ready to go, honey?"

She nodded and let them lead her out of the shop and across the street to where they'd moved the transport. Evidently while she'd been waiting on them, they'd gone ring hunting. They'd surprised her with the ring. Had they picked out anything else, she'd have probably refused to wear it. Instead, they'd chosen something she couldn't refuse. It looked just like the rings her parents had worn to the day they died.

* * * *

"Look at her," Porter whispered. "She's worn out."

Edward chuckled. "She probably tried on half the store at that shop. If Anna hadn't been married, I might have kissed her for how she made Hannah feel. She had fun."

"She really thinks she's too big?" Porter asked again looking down at where their woman's head lay against his shoulder.

"Yeah. I don't get it. She's perfect. I love how good she feels in my arms and the fact that I can hold on to her at night."

"You know how people are. There's always someone who has to try and tear someone else down to make themselves feel better. I love her just like she is. I don't want her to change, but if she does, it won't make any difference. She's here with us and is giving us a son. I'd care about her for that alone," Porter told the other man.

"I agree. I can't wait to see the underwear on her. I hope she wakes up enough that we can convince her to try on at least one pair for us," Edward said glancing over at her.

Porter smiled. She wasn't going to be very happy about the underwear, but he'd compromised and gotten her some plain cotton ones for working. He knew from experience that sweating in the hot sun while wearing silk boxers wasn't a pleasant experience. While he wanted to see her all decked out in the sexy silks, he didn't want her uncomfortable. The special ones were for playtime.

"I sure am glad I let you talk me out of that pretty diamond ring," Edward was saying. "The one you picked out seemed to have meant something to her. How did you know?"

"I didn't. It just looked like her. She likes things simple and honest. You're right though. It did seem to mean something to her.

We lucked out on this round." Porter brushed a light kiss over her hair before looking out around them to make sure they weren't blindsided by something.

"We go to work tomorrow. I don't like leaving her at the house all alone," Edward said several quiet minutes later.

"Me either. We need to teach her gun basics tomorrow and spend a little time every day after work having her practice," Porter agreed. "And we need to make sure she knows how to use the radio and call for help if she needs it."

"Good point. I'd forgotten about the radio. I'm still getting used to not having cell phones." Edward shook his head. "Even when we were learning about the dangers we faced while we were on the shuttle, I never really considered our wife would be alone and on her own for so much of each day. I don't like leaving her, Porter."

"Cam and Phillip said that once we got things going we could take turns working half days. That's what they do."

Edward shrugged. "Still isn't enough. There are two of us. One of us should be able to stay around the house in case of trouble. I thought that was the entire reason for two men for every woman."

"That's the plan for when there are more of us, but there's barely enough food produced now to hold everyone through the winter. Part of the cultivation has to be used for hay and grain for the cattle as well," he reminded Edward.

"Any idea on how we're going to handle being daddies?" Edward asked after another long stretch of silence.

Porter chuckled quietly. "Not a clue. I'm just praying to be able to handle diaper duty when it's my turn. I managed to get out of that particularly nasty chore when I was around my nieces and nephews back on Earth. I doubt I'll get that lucky here."

"Not if I have anything to say about it you won't," Edward muttered.

* * * *

Something tickled her neck causing her to shrug her shoulders against it. She didn't want to get up yet. She was sleeping so well. The sensation of air whispered across her earlobe just before something wet and hot closed over it. Hannah came awake with a shriek.

"Easy, baby girl. It's just me." Porter chuckled as she shivered all over.

"What are you doing?" She looked around and realized she was in the transport and they'd pulled up outside their home.

"Waking you up. If you're too tired to walk, I'll carry you, but I'd like to get unloaded as soon as possible so you've got to wake up, lazy bones." His *ouch* when she popped him on the shoulder sounded wimpy to her.

"I can walk. Help me out of this thing," she said, pulling at the harness securing her to the seat. "Where's Edward?"

"He just carried a load inside. He'll be back in a second."

"I can't believe I slept all the way back." She yawned and stretched before scooting closer to the door so Porter could swing her down from the buggy.

"Let's go," he said, holding the rifle as they walked at a fast pace across the deep blue grass to the porch.

Once inside, Hannah headed directly to the kitchen. She was starving and so thirsty she wasn't sure if there was enough of the stone berry lemonade to quench her parched throat. Had she been snoring?

By the time the guys had finished unloading, she had dinner on the table and a new batch of stone berry lemonade made up. She was seriously thinking about keeping two pitchers of the stuff in the fridge now.

"Something sure smells good," Edward said, taking his seat at the table.

"It's just something quick tonight. I don't know why I'm so tired when I slept all the way back from the space station." She sat down and they passed the food around the table.

Oddly enough, once she'd eaten half of the food on her plate, she wasn't hungry any longer. She had thought she was going to starve before she got it ready. What was going on? Maybe she just had to get used to the weird atmosphere on Alpha and it was affecting her strangely. The next time she talked to someone, she'd ask about it. Maybe she could talk to Lacy on the radio the next day about it.

"Are you finished, Hannah?" Edward asked when she sat back in the chair.

"Yeah. I think my eyes were bigger than my stomach tonight. Either that or I filled up on the stone berry lemonade when I first got back. I was dying of thirst and drank two full glasses, one right after the other."

"We should keep something to drink with us when we head out anywhere and plan to be gone longer than an hour, especially in the summer," Porter suggested. "I didn't even think about it. I'm sorry, baby."

"I didn't think about it either. It's not your fault." She stood up and picked up her plate to carry it to the sink.

"Are you sure you've had enough? You really didn't eat that much and you didn't eat much at lunch," Edward said.

"I can always get a snack later if I get hungry. I'm full though."

As she washed the dishes and cleaned up, Hannah kept looking at her ring and wanted to tell them again how much she appreciated it. Tears pricked her eyelids once again as she remembered how much her mother had loved her Celtic love knot ring. Her father wore one just like it but wider. She couldn't help but wonder if she could get one made for each of her men. Then she remembered that they weren't on Earth any longer. There wouldn't be anyone to create or make things like that now. They would be more interested in making useful things, not frivolous jewelry.

Once she'd finished the kitchen, Hannah wondered into the living room to find both men sitting in their respective loungers talking about the strain of grain they were going to be planting in the next few days. When she settled on the couch with a book she'd brought with her they each smiled or winked at her but continued talking. It felt comfortable to sit there and read while they talked. She hadn't felt this way since her parents had been gone.

"Hannah? Honey? Did you hear what I said?" Edward asked with a soft laugh.

"No. I'm sorry." She looked over at where he still sat in his chair. She wondered how long she'd been reading or daydreaming, really.

"I asked if you were ready to model some of the clothes you got today."

She frowned. "But I already showed you all of them when I was trying them on in the store."

"Not those, baby girl. The ones I picked out at that first store," Porter said in a husky voice.

"I–I didn't realize you'd gotten anything," she said, the idea of what he might have picked out worrying her.

"Oh, I chose a few things for you to wear just for us, sweet thing," he said with a devious smile.

"I'm not sure I'm going to like this," she said, standing up. "Where did you put them?"

"On the bed. We'll wait for you down here. I think watching you parade down the stairs will be a treat indeed," Porter told her.

She risked a glance in Edward's direction and the sight of him licking his lips had her panties soaked. She'd never gotten wet like that just from the way a man seemed to anticipate looking at her. She prayed that whatever outfit Porter had chosen it would fit and she wouldn't look like a pig shoved into a cellophane wrap. It would be hard enough to model something intimate in front of them despite the fact that they'd seen all of her, up close and personal already.

As soon as she walked into the bedroom Hannah knew she was in trouble. Porter had chosen more than a couple of pairs of panties. He'd picked out at least four complete outfits along with a few negligees. She had to give him credit for also picking out several changes of comfortable cotton underwear she could work in. Still, the lacy barely there outfits scandalized her. Going naked wasn't nearly as uncomfortable as the peekaboo selections he'd gotten her.

I'm going to look like a country cousin trying to dress up when I don't know the first thing about being sexy.

Hannah sighed and fingered the silky material of a pretty pale pink bustier with matching garters. There was nothing for it except to see if they fit. She had been surprised to see that they did appear to be in her size. She debated on wearing the one pair of heels that had made it to Alpha with her but decided not to chance them on the stairs when she was already tired.

Once she'd smoothed the stockings on and double-checked to be sure everything looked okay, Hannah walked down the hall to the stairs and cleared her throat to get the guys' attention. Nothing was said as she slowly walked down the staircase in her stocking feet. She paused at the bottom and waited for them to say something.

After what felt like an eternity, Edward stood up and crossed the floor in swift strides to pick her up and throw her over his shoulder before hurrying up the stairs.

"Hey! Where are you taking her? I wanted to see her turn a few times," Porter called out not far behind them.

"Screw that. I'm so fucking hard now a few turns would be embarrassing," he said.

Hannah couldn't stop the giggle from erupting at his blunt admission. She'd never thought anyone would feel that way about her before. It was thrilling and a little scary at the same time to have a man that turned on.

"Don't rip anything, Edward," Porter all but growled as she found herself dropped on the bed to stare up at the other man.

Edward's light blue eyes sparkled a shade darker than normal as he raked them up and down her body. The intense expression on his face was more than a little jarring to Hannah. She'd never had a man look at her quite like that before.

"I swear I can smell your pussy from here. I can see how wet you are. The wet spot between your legs has my dick in a twist. If I don't get inside of you soon I'm going to go up in flames," Edward said, his voice harsh and guttural.

"I want a taste of her before you fuck her blind, Ed. She's going to taste so damn good." Porter went to his knees at the side of the bed and reached for her panties.

"Leave the stockings and garters on," Edward rasped out.

Hannah looked from where Porter was rolling her underwear down up to where Edward was already peeling out of his clothes. Her mouth watered at the sight of his thick cock throbbing in time to his heartbeat. She wanted to taste that little drop of pre-cum resting in the slit. She licked her lips and caught him looking at her mouth.

"Please?" she begged, dropping her eyes back down to where he'd fisted his dick.

"Hell, yeah." Edward climbed on the bed next to her head and held his shaft in a tight grip next to her mouth.

She reached out with the tip of her tongue and ran it along the slit to scoop up the salty essence, closing her eyes as she savored it with a sigh. His taste exploded in her mouth and she knew she had to have more. With that single thought, Hannah reached up and wrapped one hand around the base of his dick below his fist and drew him toward her open mouth. Anticipation drew a whimper from her throat as he playfully fought her pull.

"Let me have it!" she finally yelled.

Chapter Eleven

Edward would have laughed at her demand had she not managed to close her mouth around the crown of his cock in that moment and squeeze all rational thought processes from him. Her hot, moist, mouth burned every synapse in his brain to the point of frying so that he couldn't have demanded she stop had he wanted her to.

The only word that made sense in his head was *more*. He wanted more of her wet, tight teasing, more of the way her moans vibrated along his shaft to tingle in his balls so that they were so sensitized that just a breath would set him off. Then she raked her nails over them and he howled with pleasure, curling his toes to hold back the instant rush of cum that threatened to erupt from his pulsing cockhead.

"Fuck her, Porter! I'm not going to make it out of this alive. She's fucking ruining me," Edward finally managed to get out.

Porter's deep laugh should have pissed him off, but the man already knew what her mouth was like. He'd been inside it several times. This was Edward's first trip down this road. Oh, hell, it wouldn't be his last.

The way she swirled her tongue around his shaft and let her teeth barely rake at the lip of the crown of his dick sent shivers down to his toes. When she sucked it was as if the hounds of hell were snapping at his heels. The suction wasn't just tight and compelling. It drew at him to the roots of his hair. The way she held his nuts in her hand, gently rolling and squeezing them while she stroked his shaft with her other hand, had him fighting not to dig his nails into her scalp any more than he already had. Her grip was nearly perfect. Women weren't normally so aggressive, but she had it so close to that tight edge of pain that he had to look to be sure it was still her hand on his dick.

He knew the moment his partner entered her. She screamed around him, sending shards of fire tingling over his cock straight to his balls. Then she sank down on his dick with her sweet mouth and swallowed him at the back of her throat, scraping her nails along the perineum between his balls and his ass and that was all she wrote.

Edward yelled, didn't scream, because men didn't scream, until his throat was raw as his balls contracted up to the point of pain and hot ribbons of cum poured from his cock so hard and for so long he was afraid he'd turn inside out from it. Then he worried that he would choke his sweet Hannah but could do nothing about it while he was so caught up in the painful pleasure of a climax unlike anything he'd ever felt.

What. The. Fuck!

Even as he slowly regained control of his body Edward still had no control of his voice. His brain felt fried with pleasure. He released the golden strands of hair he'd gripped tightly in his hands and smoothed them down as he pulled from her mouth, afraid of what he'd see. Scared that he'd choked her, frightened her with his loss of control. Instead, when he finally looked down into her upturned face, he saw—happiness, joy. It floored him.

"Are you okay? Did I hurt you?" he managed to rasp out.

"No, I mean I'm fine. That was amazing," she said.

He looked over to where Porter stood between her legs, massaging her outer thighs as he watched them. He'd stopped fucking her at some point. Probably to keep from shoving her throat down over his dick.

Looking back down at the amazing woman still smiling up at him, Edward knew she was perfect for them and that God or fate had planned for her to be theirs. He could feel the first tinges of love growing in his heart for her.

"Thank you, honey. I've never felt anything like what you just gave me." He soothed his thumb over her swollen lips the color of cherries.

"Let's take care of our wife, Edward," Porter said in a soft voice with the barest hint of strain in it.

Edward looked up and smiled. "My pleasure."

With that, he stretched out on his side and kissed Hannah as he ran the pads of his thumb over one peaked nipple. Her slight gasp into his mouth had him smiling. He wanted to give her just as much pleasure if not more than she'd just given him. His balls still ached with the force of his ejaculation.

Her deep moan reminded him that he had help in taking care of her with Porter easing in and out of her hot cunt. He knew firsthand how good that felt. Her tight muscles sucking at your dick while you sank balls deep inside of her was enough to make him hard again. His groan joined hers and Porter's.

Edward moved his mouth from hers to nip at her chin then kiss his way down her throat and around to her neck. There he sucked and licked, enjoying the salty taste of her excitement before moving lower to capture one ripe berry between his teeth. He squeezed her breast so that it forced more of the tight bud upward for him to suck on. Her gasp of pleasure told him all he needed to know as he ran the tip of his tongue around her hard nipple. Without giving her ease he moved to the other one and treated it with the same teasing moves.

"Oh, God! Please. I need to come." Hannah's plea had his cock stirring all over again.

"We'll take care of you, honey. Just feel how hot it gets when you have to wait," he said.

"No, no, no. Please don't tease me," she pleaded.

Hearing her beg for release was the sweetest sound. Their sweet demure Hannah could ask for what she wanted. He lightly bit her nipple then sucked it hard against the roof of his mouth as he plucked at the other tender bud. Fingers dug into his hair, holding him tightly against her breast as he sucked and pinched.

"Fuck!" Porter's shouted cry confirmed that Hannah had exploded around the man.

Edward had her hands kneading his scalp as his ears rang with the keening cry of her orgasm. Knowing that he'd help give her that pleasure thrilled him, made him proud to be a man. He'd never thought about it before, though he'd always made sure the woman he was with found her release. Now it was a point of pride to know that he'd given her what she needed or at least part of it.

"Hell, she's going to squeeze my dick off," Porter rasped out.

Edward released the nipple from his mouth and looked up to see the exquisite torturous pleasure filling Porter's face as the man came with a cry. It reminded him of his own explosive release of earlier and his cock jerked in response. Hannah was amazing, simply amazing, and she was all theirs.

* * * *

Hannah lay flat on her back, panting as Porter collapsed next to her after pulling from her pussy. She'd come so hard and so long that her muscles were cramping in her ass cheeks. She moaned and tried to move to relive the tight pain.

"What is it, honey?" Edward asked, concern on his face.

"Butt cramps," she hissed out.

He chuckled, but rolled her over and started massaging her buttocks. It hurt at first but soon smoothed out to feel much better. She sighed.

"Thanks. That's better."

Porter laughed next to her. "I gather that you came pretty hard."

She giggled and smoothed her hand over his chest. While he had a smidgen of chest hair, it wasn't enough to really dig her fingers in. Still, she managed to find enough to pull a few hairs.

"Ouch!"

Edward spanked her ass with a laugh. "You've got some hair we can pull, too, you know."

"Sorry, Porter." She instantly wanted to cover her pussy with her hands.

"You're perfect, Hannah," Edward suddenly said out of the blue.

She smiled. Hearing him say that sent chills down her spine. It was a start and she wanted it to grow. When she opened her mouth to tell him that he was super too, her brain short circuited and that wasn't what came out.

"I'm hungry," she said instead.

Both men laughed so hard the bed shook. She frowned. Where had that come from? She hadn't meant to say that.

"Let's go fix our woman something to eat. She's eating for two now," Porter said with a grin.

Hannah frowned, still unsure why she'd blurted out that she was hungry like that. Yeah, she was hungry, but not excessively so like she'd inferred. Shaking her head, she climbed out of bed behind the men and padded to the bathroom. Once she'd cleaned up some, Hannah walked downstairs to find the men busy in the kitchen putting together some of the native fruit and cheese plate.

"Juice to drink or tea?" Edward asked.

She started to say juice, but milk came out instead. She never drank milk.

"Good for you, baby girl," Porter said. "The baby needs milk for strong bones."

She shrugged, deciding that her body knew what she needed and she might as well accept that she wasn't going to get what she wanted until after the baby was born. After all, that was the reason behind strange cravings. When you craved something, it was your body's way of obtaining some vitamin or nutrient it was lacking.

By the time they'd finished eating the snack the men had put together, Hannah was wide awake again. She was glad she'd gotten her second wind. There was a pile of clothes upstairs to put away. Deciding it wouldn't be in her best interests to advertise what she was going to do, Hannah left the men discussing the issues of pollination without bugs or birds. She'd never thought about that before. She'd just been excited to find out that there weren't any on Alpha. Now she couldn't help but wonder how all of the flowers and trees and weeds continued spreading.

By the time she made it to the second floor, Hannah's second wind had petered out. She had to force herself to put away her new clothes and made a half-assed attempt at straightening the covers before she climbed back in the bed. She'd just rest her eyes for a few minutes then get up and clean up the mess in the bathroom. Somehow, she managed to scramble beneath the covers and settle down for the night so that when the men came to bed later she roused enough to realize it was late.

"What time is it?" she asked with a yawn.

"Nearly one in the morning, honey. Sorry we woke you," Edward said brushing a light kiss across her lips. "Go on back to sleep."

"Bathroom first," she mumbled rolling over to crawl out on Porter's side. He was still sitting on the side of the bed pulling off his boots.

"Careful there, baby girl. You're not fully awake. I don't want you to fall."

She grumbled something about being fine and hurried to the bathroom to relieve herself. Once there, Hannah decided to wash her face and brush her teeth. She hadn't gotten around to that earlier since she hadn't planned on falling asleep. She sure hoped those prenatal vitamins and the extra iron would help her regain some energy. She was less than a week along in the pregnancy and already had no stamina. Weren't pregnant women supposed to get some burst of vitality with a nesting instinct or something?

She harrumphed at that. So far the only nesting she felt like doing dealt with bed covers and a comfy mattress. On her way back to bed, she suddenly decided she needed something to drink. Was she thirsty? Yeah, she was thirsty.

The men appeared to already have fallen asleep. She slipped on her house shoes and tiptoed out the door and down the hall. By the time she'd made it downstairs to the kitchen, her mouth was dry and that drink sounded even better than it had upstairs. This time she pulled out the pitcher of juice and poured a big glassful before replacing it in the fridge.

Hannah wondered over to the window and gazed out at the two huge moons that illuminated the yard outside. She couldn't see the garden from there, but she could see the various plants and grass just outside the window. There must have been a breeze because it all looked as if were moving. She could have sworn that she was watching it grow but couldn't see how that would be possible. Things just didn't grow that fast.

When she looked down at the ground to focus on one of the plants, a pair of orange eyes peered up at her from only a few inches from the edge of the porch. Hannah nearly dropped the glass she was holding and did take a step back.

"What the…"

She leaned closer to the window and studied the creature looking back at her. It didn't look like a muskie or dorrie based on the pictures she'd seen in books. This looked more like a cross between a long, smooth pig and a platypus. Its hairless skin was the color of a yellow duckling and it stretched to be about five feet from the tip of its rounded ears to its two stubby tails, or what she assumed were tails.

It had a very flat and long nose and mouth combination that was almost like a duck's bill, but it wasn't hard, and it moved more like a mouth than a beak. The thing stared up at her with what looked like curiosity to her. The shiny orange glow of its eyes was unnerving but it didn't show her any teeth. She wondered if it had teeth or not.

Just as it turned and waddled off, she realized that she should have gotten the camera they had and taken a picture. Had she seen something no one else had ever seen before? The idea excited her. She wanted to go wake up the men and tell them about her discovery but figured it could wait until morning. They were tired and the strange creature had already been swallowed up in the dark shadows of the yard. Oddly enough, having two moons seemed to increase the number and depth of the shadows. If something was tall, they illuminated it much better, but close to the ground or near an object that cast a shadow and there seemed to be even less light than normal.

Hannah was convinced that she'd made a unique discovery and decided to write down a description of it while her memory was fresh. The sighting had given her a spurt of energy she hadn't had earlier. Setting the glass down, she hurried to the office and located a pencil and paper. For the next twenty minutes or so, she recorded her memory of the creature then attempted to draw parts of it for good measure. When she had finished, the drawing looked comical, but fairly accurate. She couldn't wait for the guys to wake up so she could tell them about the weird animal.

I wonder if they'll let me name it. Even if they don't, I can call it what I want to, anyway.

With that defiant thought, Hannah put everything away except her notes and drawings and turned off the lights. Then she climbed the stairs to ease back into the bedroom, careful not to wake up the guys. She thought she'd succeeded until Edward softly patted her bare ass as she settled under the covers between him and Porter.

"Where have you been, honey?" he asked in a sleepy voice.

"I was thirsty. I'll tell you in the morning." She snuggled with her ass against him and wrapped one arm over Porter's broad shoulder.

"Um, hm," was all he said before a soft snore let her know he'd fallen back asleep.

Hannah smiled and closed her eyes. Everything was really going to be okay. She had two men who obviously cared about her and she had no trouble falling asleep with that thought firmly in her thoughts with that thought firmly in her thoughts.

Chapter Twelve

"I've never seen anything like this before," Porter said, staring at the drawing Hannah had created. He read back over her description then shook his head.

"We need to see if anyone else has seen something like it before. Maybe since she saw it in the middle of the night, it's nocturnal, so it just hasn't been seen yet. This planet is huge, there's no way we've seen even a tenth of the animal life here," Edward said.

"We can take the drawing with us tomorrow when we start work. Today we need to be sure everything is ready for her to be on her own for the day," Porter said, setting the papers on the cabinet.

"We'll start out with learning how to use the radio then move on to gun safety," Edward said with a nod. "Let's go, honey. I'm anxious to get to the gun part."

Hannah felt the tension in the air the moment she'd shown them the drawing and told them about the strange-looking creature she'd seen. Both men had instantly gone into protect mode. While cute and comforting, it was also a bit suffocating. Both men had closed in on her and kept them between her while she'd been washing and putting away the breakfast dishes. She was sure it was subconscious on their part. Who needed to be protected in the house while washing dishes?

She let them usher her back to the office where the radio base was located. There were three handheld radios as well. She knew she would be keeping one near her while the guys had the other two.

A thought bothered her though. How far would they reach? She picked one of them up and turned to Edward.

"How far will these reach? I mean if I need you, will you be close enough to hear me?" she asked.

"Sometimes we won't be within reach on the mobiles but if you use the base station, you will almost always be able to reach us. Even if you can't get us, you can reach someone with the base station. We're going to show you all the frequencies and how to set them. The list is right here for you to follow," Porter said pointing to a list of numbers with names out by them.

Hannah frowned. It all looked much too complicated to her. How would she ever remember everything?

"Hey, baby girl. Don't look so worried. You'll get it. Just relax and watch." Porter squeezed her shoulder and sat her down in the chair in front of the base unit.

Over the next hour, they taught her how to change channels and dial different frequencies to reach different places like the clinic at the space station and their individual hand units. She put a star out beside them as well as Lacy's so she could call the other woman to ask questions. All of a sudden, she didn't feel quite so lonely now that she understood how to use the radio.

"Now for gun safety lessons," Edward said.

Hannah wasn't too thrilled about this next part. She didn't like guns, never had. They frightened much more than she'd ever admitted to anyone. Maybe if she told them they wouldn't make her touch one, but one look at Porter and she knew they would still insist. The determination to make sure she was safe was etched in stone across his brow.

They had her look at the rifles and the two handguns that they had and explained the differences in them. Then Edward picked up one of the rifles and showed her all of the features before having her hold it. The entire time she had to keep from screaming that she didn't want to touch it. She knew on a gut level that it was for her safety, and now her unborn child's safety, that she learn how to handle one. Still, it didn't make it easy.

"Now. Show me where the safety is," Porter said. When she pointed it out, he nodded. "Good. Now show me how to take the safety off."

For the next thirty minutes, she located the safety and flicked it on and off on each of the guns. Then they moved on to show her how to safely carry each of them. Porter told her that having respect for them was paramount. If she remembered that they could kill at all times, she'd be more likely to remain safe.

"Remember. Even if you just unloaded them yourself, you always treat a gun like it's loaded," Edward added. "Accidents can happen. You could leave one bullet in without realizing it. Never point it at anything you don't intend to pull the trigger on."

"I think we're ready for target practice now," Porter said with a wink.

"Um, can we wait until after lunch? I'm hungry and my arms are tired from picking them up and down," she hedged.

They didn't seem to realize it was more a ploy to put off the inevitable since they quickly nodded and steered her toward the kitchen.

"Sorry, baby girl. I didn't think about how heavy they would feel to you. We'll make something for lunch. You sit down and rest your arms. We don't want to wear you out." Porter shoved her into a chair before kissing her loudly on the lips.

"I can fix sandwiches, guys. I'm not that tired," she said with a chuckle.

"We can throw something together, Hannah. Just rest." Edward and Porter converged at the fridge and mumbled to each other as she sat watching in amusement.

Throw something together? Right. This was going to be interesting.

She had no doubt that both men could take care of themselves if they had to, but with the limited possibilities on Alpha, whatever they came up with was bound to be interesting. She just hoped she was able to eat it. She didn't want to hurt their feelings when they were being so nice.

She was pleasantly surprised though when they made sandwiches from the leftover roast she'd cooked the day before. It meant she would need to make more bread though. They were running low. Actually, she was looking forward to that. Making bread was a relaxing activity to her. Kneading the dough and shaping it into a perfect loaf always made her feel as if she'd accomplished something.

"What are you thinking about, Hannah? You've got a dreamy expression on your face," Edward said.

"She's thinking about me," Porter said with a wide grin.

"She'd look like she was in pain if she was thinking about you," Edward said.

"Actually, I was thinking about making bread. I'll need to make two or three loafs each time I make it with the way you two eat," she teased.

Edward shook his head. "I'll never understand women."

"You're not supposed to understand them, Ed. You're just supposed to accept them and keep them happy," Porter said.

"I like that idea," she said with a laugh.

"Okay, time for target practice." Edward stood up and pulled her to her feet.

"Let me clean up the dishes first," she protested.

"They'll keep. There's just a few plates and knives. Won't hurt them to sit here till we get through," Porter pointed out. "You're stalling."

"I don't like guns."

"You've told us that several times already, honey. I think we get the picture. The thing is, you have to be able to shoot one to protect yourself. What if we're not around?" Edward asked with a frown.

She just sighed and followed the two men out the back door. Learning how to shoot wasn't something she'd ever aspired to learning when she was growing up, but she understood that in her present situation, it was a necessary evil. So be it. She'd learn to shoot and pray she never had to actually shoot at anything.

To her astonishment and that of her two men, Hannah was a natural at it. After a stumbling start with remembering how to flip off the safety and aim, she grazed or hit pretty much all of the targets the men had set up for her.

"Well, well," Edward crooned. "We've got ourselves a little Annie Oakley in the making."

"Can we stop now?" was all she asked.

They both chuckled and together, they gathered up the assorted weapons and ammunition to carry it inside.

"Remember. A rifle will always be by the back door and you keep one of the pistols with you at all times," Porter said. "We'll keep one of our rifles at the front door when we're home."

"I've got it. What are we going to do when we run out of bullets?" she asked as they put everything away.

"They're working on modifying our weapons to handle something they've found here on Alpha. Don't know anything about it yet, but they're working on it at the space station." Porter ruffled her hair.

"I'm about ready for a nap. What about you, precious?" Edward asked.

She looked over at the odd clock designed to keep time on Alpha. It was close to two in the afternoon and it wouldn't get dark until close to eight. They weren't even in the longer days that marked summer yet, but with the extra hour, it tended to stay light longer here.

"I could probably use a nap," she admitted. "Or is that code for having sex with you guys?" she asked with a smile.

"Oh, our Hannah is getting a little frisky on us, Ed." Porter dove for her and wrapped his arms around her before she could move away.

"Hey, put me down." She tried for indignant, but the giggle at the end sort of ruined it.

"Hold on, baby girl. We're going for a ride." Porter carted her out of the office and up the stairs with Edward following close behind them. He winked at her as Porter carried her into the bedroom.

When the big man gently laid her on the bed, she started to scoot over to the center of the bed, but Edward stopped her, wrapping his hands around her ankles and holding her still. She frowned and looked down her body at where he knelt at the foot of the bed and stared up at her.

"What are you doing?" she asked.

"He's holding you still so I can have my evil way with you. Now be quiet. I want to talk to our son." Porter knelt on the floor next to the bed and pulled her top up to expose her rounded belly.

"But he's only a few days along. I doubt he can hear you or anything, yet," she protested.

"We don't know what he can hear or understand. We plan to talk to him every day until he's born, so get used to it." Porter leaned over and unfastened her jeans to pull them and her panties a few inches down.

"Hey there, little fellow. This is your daddy, Porter. Your daddy, Edward, will talk to you in a minute. I know you're only a few days old in there, but we want to make sure you recognize us when you're born." Porter kissed her belly sending soft chills along her spine.

Hannah couldn't help but tear up at how he caressed her belly as he talked. How had she gotten so lucky? The two big men were so sweet and caring. Despite how they'd started off and despite her insecurities, they had proved over and over that they cared about her and were dedicated to making things work. She couldn't have asked for better men to be hers.

"Now you behave yourself in there and don't be making your momma sick or anything. We'll talk again later, sport. Here's Daddy Ed to talk to you now." Porter moved over an Edward scooted around to take his place.

The first thing he did was blow a raspberry on her tummy making her curl up and giggle.

"Stop that! You're going to scare him and make me pee on myself!" she gasped.

"Naw. Hey there, butterbean. It's Daddy Edward and we're going to have a great time when you get here. In the meantime, grow big and strong for us, son. We'll look out for you while you're incubating in there."

"Not too big. I have to be able to have him, Edward. And stop talking to him like's he's a baby chicken or something." She tried to glare at him, but somehow, seeing him on his knees talking to her belly took away her starch. He looked so cute like that.

"He's not a chicken. He's a strong stallion who'll grow up to be big and strong like his two dads," Edward said with a grin. He petted her tummy. "Isn't that right, son?"

She shook her head and sat up enough that she could prop up on her elbows. "Look, you two. That's enough. We all need a nap. That includes the baby. Would one of you help me with my shoes?"

They each took a shoe and removed it then continued on to remove her jeans but left her in her panties. Next came her shirt and they insisted that her bra accompany the shirt to the floor.

"It can't be comfortable to sleep in it. Just relax now and we'll give you a rubdown to relax you," Edward said.

Porter kissed her on the nose before lightly brushing his hands up and down her arms while Edward started with her feet. After a while, Hannah couldn't think. Her eyes had long since closed and the soft barely-there touches seemed to blend in with her heartbeat. Then she drifted off to sleep and dreamed of her child talking to her inside of her belly.

* * * *

"I don't think she's ever going to wake up." Edward's voice seemed to be coming from a thousand miles away as she floated in a sea of soft Jell-O. It was her favorite flavor, too—strawberry.

"Wake up, sleepyhead. If you don't wake up now, you'll be wide awake all night." She recognized Porter's voice that time and it was much, much closer.

One eye popped open and she realized he needed to shave. He had a shadow of a beard along his jawline. She wondered what time it was and then groaned as her other eye popped open at the realization that she needed to get up. She was only supposed to take a short nap. How long had she been asleep?

"W–what time is it?"

"It's nearly six. You've been a sleep forever, baby girl. How are you feeling?" Porter backed off the bed.

"Like I've been drinking. I'm not usually so groggy when I take a nap. I feel like I still want to sleep for a while longer," she said rolling to her side.

"Better get up though. I want you to be able to sleep tonight," Edward told her. "Let's take a walk and you can watch us while we water the garden and check the fence line."

"A little exercise will be good for you," Porter added with a grin.

She slapped at his hip halfheartedly but stood up and focused on remaining that way. She really did feel a little post drunk. The next thing she knew, she was making a beeline to the bathroom and emptying her already empty stomach.

"Easy, baby girl. We've got you." Porter held her hair out of the way as she heaved over and over again.

"Here." Edward's voice sounded a little ill. "I'm glad you've got her."

Porter ran a cool wet cloth over her face and then behind her neck. "Give me another one, man."

She heard the water in the sink turn on then another cold wet cloth rested against her forehead. She sighed in relief. It felt so good to her heated skin.

"How's that?" Porter asked softly.

"Good. Thanks." She wanted to get off her knees, but was afraid to move.

"Just rest for a few seconds then I'll help you get up. I guess morning sickness for you is afternoon." Porter's voice remained soft near her ear.

"I don't like being sick," she said with a pout.

"I know, baby. I know."

"I'm going to go get her some juice to help settle her stomach," Edward said from somewhere on the other side of Porter. She heard his footsteps fade away.

"Poor thing. He can't handle you throwing up. Don't know if it's the gagging or just that you're sick," Porter said with a soft chuckle.

"*I* can't handle me getting sick."

"Let's see if you can stand up now." Porter stood up but remained bent over to help her to her feet. "Easy does it, baby. I've got you."

She slowly stood upright with Porter's hand at her back. He removed the two wet cloths and helped her shuffle to the sink where she rinsed her mouth then tried toothpaste and found she couldn't handle it yet.

"You can brush your teeth after the nausea has passed," he said.

"You need to have a talk with your son. I can't get sick like this anymore," she said only half kidding.

"We'll have a talk once your belly has settled down. I'm sure Edward will want to have his say as well."

"About what?" Edward walked in with a glass of the stone berry lemonade she favored.

Porter chuckled. "She wants us to talk to the little fella about not making her sick anymore."

"I'm all for that," Edward said with a grimace. "I can't stand seeing you get sick. Plus, it makes me gag with you."

She arched a brow at him. "I think it's only fair that if I have to get sick, you should, too."

"Then who's going to get you something to drink afterward?" he asked with a quick smile.

"Don't worry, baby girl. If he gets sick when you do, I'll take care of you." Porter hugged her from behind as she sipped at her juice.

She smiled at him through their reflection in the mirror. Edward joined them and gently rubbed her belly. She took a mental picture of them like that, planning to remember this moment forever. Despite having been ill, it was a nearly perfect point in time for them. Hannah couldn't remember ever feeling happier. The only thing that would make it perfect was to have her sister there as well.

She shoved that thought to the back of her mind. No sense wishing for things she couldn't have and dwelling on it would only remind her of the ticking timer that was Earth.

"I'm hungry." She frowned. Where had that come from? She'd just finished being sick.

Porter and Edward both burst out laughing. Their hands dropped away.

"Why don't you get cleaned up and dressed while we fix something to eat?" Porter said.

"It's my turn. I'm supposed to be cooking the meals, not the two of you," she said.

"Don't worry, honey." Edward took her now empty glass from her. "We're going to be depending on you to keep us fed once we start work tomorrow."

At that reminder, Hannah sighed. She hated that they had so little time to get to know each other before they had to be gone all day every day. Most newly married couples got at least a week for their honeymoon. Instead of moping about it, she hurried through getting cleaned up and dressed. When she walked into the kitchen twenty minutes later, the men were nowhere to be found. She looked out the window but didn't see them out back. Maybe they were in the office. She started to head in that direction, but something stopped her. She really was hungry—extremely hungry.

Without thinking about it, she turned back around and returned to the kitchen. They had warmed up some soup of some kind. She pulled out some soda bread and dipped up a bowl of the creamy liquid.

I don't think the guys will mind if I start without them.

She sat at the table and started eating. She couldn't remember being this ravenous before.

"Hey there, baby girl. Couldn't wait for us?" Porter walked in and dropped a kiss on her head before walking to the stove.

"Sorry. I wasn't sure where you were and all of a sudden I was starved!" she told him.

"I'm going to call you our little piggy," Edward teased.

"No fair. It's not my fault," she said with a frown.

"Then instead of butterbean, we'll call the baby piggy until he's born. Better start thinking of some names or baby piggy might stick," Edward said.

Porter sat down next to her and reached for the container of soda bread. Before she knew what she was doing, Hannah growled at him. She gasped and nearly choked on the mouthful of soup she'd just taken.

"Hey! Are you okay?" Porter patted her on the back and stared at her with concern.

"Yeah. I'm sorry. I don't know why I growled like that." She was sure her face had turned a bright pink.

He just laughed. "You can growl at me anytime, baby. I'll ask next time before I steal your crackers."

Edward sat down across from her with a thoughtful expression on his face. She wondered what he was thinking, but soon forgot about it as she resumed eating. The soup was delicious. She thought she'd need another bowl but by the time she'd finished the one in front of her, she was satisfied.

"Did you get enough?" Edward asked.

"I'm full. Thanks guys. The soup was really good. I'll clean up." She stood up and carried her bowl and spoon over to the sink.

"I'm going to get some more tea, Hannah. Do you want more juice?" Edward asked.

"Yes, thanks. I stay so thirsty for some reason."

"Must be the baby," Porter suggested. "When are you supposed to take the vitamins? In the morning or at night?"

"In the mornings. I took them this morning. The iron pill is nasty. I wasn't sure I was going to get it down," she confessed.

The guys chatted with her while she washed up. Edward even put away the dishes once she'd dried them. It felt so normal to spend time talking while she cleaned up the kitchen. Hannah was thankful for Edward and Porter. They could have rejected her or at the very least, made her miserable after what she'd done to them, but they hadn't held it against her. If it took the rest of her life, she would make sure she thanked them over and over for accepting her.

"I don't know about you guys, but I think I want to sit in the living room and relax for a while before bedtime," Edward said.

"Me too." Hannah wanted to read some more. "I almost hate to finish my book, but it's at a good part."

"We can get more books from the space station when we go back next time, baby. I didn't even think about it when we were there the other day." Porter followed her into the living room where Edward had already stretched out on one of the recliners.

"What kind of books do you like, honey?" Edward asked.

"Just about any kind. I love mysteries and suspense," she admitted.

"I would have thought you'd be all over the romance books," Porter teased her.

"I am, but not all the time. Plus, a lot of romance books have mystery and suspense in them."

"Yeah, in between the sex scenes," Edward said.

She started to throw her pillow at him but decided she needed it to prop her up instead. She just stuck her tongue out at him.

"Oh, honey. You keep that up and we'll be heading on upstairs instead of relaxing down here," he said.

She giggled but rolled her eyes at him. The easy banter between the three of them settled around her like a warm comfy sweater. Hannah smiled and opened her book. It wasn't long before she was immersed in the plot and time fell away.

When Edward tapped her head several times, Hannah frowned up at him.

"What?"

He chuckled. "We've been trying to get your attention for the last fifteen minutes, honey. That book must be really good. Porter even offered to suck your toes if you'd come to bed."

"Oh. I'm sorry. I never heard you. I guess I was really into the book." She smiled even though she could feel the heat spread across her face.

"He went on upstairs to run a bath for you. We figured you would enjoy relaxing in one before bed," Edward told her as he helped her to her feet.

"I can't believe you've been talking to me and I didn't hear you. That's really not like me." Hannah thought back to the book. It was a very good book, not her usual romantic suspense, but a straight murder mystery with a lot of military jargon in it.

She let Edward lead her upstairs and enjoyed the teasing as he helped her undress. Twice he licked her nipple sending sparks straight to her clit. When he squeezed her ass cheeks, Hannah couldn't wait to finish her bath and climb into bed with the two men. Her hormones seemed to be in overdrive.

"There she is," Porter said with a stern expression. "Ignore me, will you? I think not. I'm going to spank that ass after your bath."

She wiggled her eyebrows at him. "Oh really? We'll see."

He growled at her as he helped her step into the massive tub. She settled in and watched as he undressed.

"Are you going to join me?" she asked.

"No. Not tonight, baby. I'm going to take a quick shower. Edward is using the other one down the hall. That way we'll all be about finished at the same time. We have an early day tomorrow," he said, reminding her that they would be going off to work.

She watched as he stepped into the shower then concentrated on bathing so she could relax until they were ready to get her out. The warm water felt so good, so relaxing. It still bothered her that she'd tuned the guys out so much so that she hadn't heard them when they were trying to get her attention. If it had been one of her naughty romance books, Hannah might have believed that she had managed to get lost in the story, but a straight suspense? It didn't make sense.

When Porter finished his shower and started toweling off, Hannah couldn't help but watch the powerful play of muscles as he chased water droplets from his skin. She longed to lick his chest dry and nearly laughed out loud at how silly that sounded. But all it took was another look at the round discs of his nipples and her mouth watered all over again. Yes, she would enjoy tasting him from head to foot.

"You keep looking at me like that, baby girl, and I'm going to pull you out of that tub right here and now," Porter said with a raspy snarl.

She hid her smile behind the bath cloth and turned away to try and regain some control of her expression. He was so hot to look at. Edward was just as good looking. Both men were drool worthy. It was no wonder that she stared when they were naked.

"She's still in the tub?" Edward's voice sounded from the bedroom. "Thought for sure you'd have her out by now, man."

"I'm working on it," Porter told the other man.

"Well, work faster. My cock has been hard since we ate. Watching her make love to that bowl of soup just about did me in."

She giggled then sobered when Edward stomped into the room and stared down at her in all of his naked glory, thick cock standing out away from his body in heavy need. She swallowed hard then looked over at where Porter fisted his in one hand. Yes, she wanted them both. Preferably together—at the same time.

She licked her lips and slowly looked up their bodies to stare into each of their eyes. Porter growled, his eyes at half-mast, awash in lust and erotic intent. Edward's face looked almost comical with the need reflected there. Hannah couldn't wait to be between them. She pulled herself up using the edge of the tub, intending to step out and dry off, but Porter stopped her, picking her up instead and setting her on the counter next to one of the sinks.

"I can't wait, precious. I've got to taste you now."

Chapter Thirteen

Porter dove between her legs, spreading them wide to accommodate his broad shoulders. Her heady scent called to him. He didn't think he'd ever wanted a woman as badly as he did Hannah. She was perfect for them. The more he got to know her, the more he knew she'd been meant for them. He just hated that they had to leave for work the next morning. There was so much more he wanted to learn about her.

The first taste of her on his tongue had him groaning with need. Already hard as petrified wood, his dick ached as he licked her from her slit to her clit. He was careful not to give her too much attention there yet. He wanted her hungry for them before he let her climax. He had to move over slightly as Edward joined in, cupping her breasts with his big hands.

Her soft moans heightened his own arousal to the point of pain. He'd never last at this rate. He needed to slow down, but Christ, how to do that with her right there, her taste on his tongue. Porter was in heaven and hadn't even died yet.

"So sweet, honey. I love the way they taste," Edward was saying.

Porter knew his friend was right about those hard little berries that sat on her breasts, but nothing tasted as good as her tangy juices, especially when she came. He couldn't wait to indulge himself in that delight again. Still, he had to make her wait for it. It would be so much better if he prolonged it for her. All he had to do was hold his own needs off for just a little longer.

Hell! That was going to be next to impossible. He wanted her like he wanted air to breathe. No way was Porter going to be able to stand it much longer. Her soft moans and the way she had the fingers of one hand gripping his hair sent tingles down his spine straight to his balls.

He glanced up and nearly lost it right there. Edward had his mouth drawing solidly on one nipple while he pinched and pulled her other nipple with his fingers. The sight of her eyes squeezed shut and her head thrown back with her little pink tongue sticking out drove him crazy. Porter gave up and sucked her clit into his mouth and rubbed over the distended numb with the tip of his tongue while holding her hips still.

She came apart under his mouth. Her exquisite juices flowed into his mouthy as she screamed in pleasure. He could feel her body shake under his hands. It was almost more than he could stand. His cock throbbed with his heartbeat. He was desperate to get inside of her.

"Move over, man. I want to taste her," Edward said with a near growl.

Porter had to bite back the refusal on his tongue. He didn't blame the other man for wanting a taste. She tasted like spicy honey. He would never be able to get enough of her if he lived to be a hundred years old. Stepping aside, he took advantage of her panting to kiss her, sweeping his tongue inside her mouth and sharing her nectar.

She immediately latched on to the invading member and drew on it like a newborn puppy. The feel of her mouth sucking him like that was nearly his undoing. It made him think of her sucking on something a little lower. Porter pulled back to keep from embarrassing himself. Her soft whimper was music to his ears. She wanted him. Knowing that made everything that much more difficult. He wanted to pull Edward away from her so they could get her to the bedroom and on the bed where it would be easier to make love to her.

As if hearing his thoughts, Edward pulled away, licking her juices from his lips and scooped her up in his arms.

"Bedroom. Now!" he said.

"About damn time," Porter muttered.

He followed the other man back into the bedroom and waited for him to settle her on the bed before they both crawled up on either side of her. Looking down at her flushed skin and the way her breasts moved as she panted, trying to slow her breathing down made him smile. She was theirs and they were giving her pleasure, padding his ego a bit.

"You've got me so hot, baby. I'm never going to get enough of you." Porter lowered his head to kiss her.

His chest ached with how sensual her moan sounded when their lips met. He sipped at them before urging her to open for him. Porter didn't waste time teasing. Instead, he devoured her like a man starved for days. The mere thought of leaving her to go work in the fields ate at him already. When had he become so possessive that he didn't want her to leave his sight? Surely it wasn't possessiveness but just an overwhelming need to be near her, keep her safe.

Love.

It was love. He loved her. The sudden knowledge had him stilling over her. How could he have fallen in love with her so fast? Was love at first sight really possible?

"Get on top of Porter, honey. Ride him, Hannah. I want to bury my cock in your tight ass." Edward's words spurred him into action as he rolled over to his back taking Hannah with him.

She laughed as she straddled his hips with her body. He loved hearing her laugh. Edward nuzzled her neck with his mouth, making her shiver. The slight movement of her body teased at his swollen cock where she had him trapped between her wet, hot pussy lips. Porter couldn't help but lift his hips to increase the friction as she slid over him.

Hell, yeah. That's so damn good.

It took every ounce of strength inside of him not to moan out loud at just how good it did feel. Instead, he complained to Edward.

"Stop messing around, man. I need to be inside her."

The other man had the nerve to laugh at him. "Feeling a little too good but not good enough?"

"Fuck you, man," Porter snapped back then buried his face between Hannah's breasts when he pulled her down to him.

Her soft giggles next to his ear had him smiling as he inhaled her heady scent. Not taking advantage of her breasts right there in his face would have been crazy, so Porter licked and sucked all over the generous mounds as he gently repositioned her so that his cockhead brushed her opening. One push. Just one small bump of his hips and he could be surrounded by all that amazing heat.

Holding back was a lot tougher than he'd thought it would be, but he wanted to see her eyes as he entered her. Seeing how her eyes widened then darkened as he sank his dick into her tight, wet cunt would be worth the strain of waiting. Maybe.

Definitely.

Porter let her slowly raise up so that they looked at each other then he tilted his pelvis and thrust upward, groaning like an old man as her pussy spread for him. Fire burned his balls as he sank deeper inside of her until finally, she rested flush against his pelvis, sitting there with her eyes so wide and glassy that she looked like a lost waif. Her cheeks were already flushed with her arousal but he knew it would spread down her neck and across her chest as they took her even higher.

It was too much and not enough all rolled up in one. Porter knew he'd have to tighten his control to keep from blowing his load before Edward had even entered her ass. Holy hell, she would be tight once the other man breached her back hole.

"Are you okay, baby?" he finally rasped out.

She nodded but moaned. Then Edward was pushing forward so that he had room to prepare her rear for his dick. He wanted to remind the other man to go slow and make sure to use plenty of the lube, but he kept silent. Edward wouldn't hurt her. He'd make sure she was ready before he did anything. Porter knew this, but the urge was still there, a result of his love for her, no doubt.

"You're so beautiful, Hannah. I love how your eyes get all bright when you're turned on," he told her as he held her in his arms.

Porter was sure Edward was preparing her tiny hole and wanted to keep her relaxed. He rubbed his lips across her chin and nipped it lightly before kissing where he'd bit.

"How are you doing, sweetness?"

"I'm hot, and I need to move. Can't be still," she said in a near moan.

"Easy, baby. We'll take care of you. Just a few more seconds." He looked over her shoulder at Edward. "About ready?"

"Just about. She's so tight, Porter. I'll never last once I get inside." Edward seemed to be panting already and he hadn't even started to enter her yet.

"Slow, man. Take it easy with her." He winced. He'd promised himself he wasn't going to say anything.

"I will. She's so tight and hot. How did you manage to hold off last time, man?" Edward asked.

"Will you two stop gossiping and do something? I'm dying here," Hannah yelled from between them.

Porter chuckled then groaned when Edward began easing his cock into Hannah's already-tight ass. Adding his girth squeezed her around Porter even more. Hell, he wanted to make it good for Hannah but at this rate, he'd be surprised if he managed a dozen strokes in and out of her sweet cunt.

"Yes!" she screamed out as Edward seemed to settle all the way inside of her. Her nails dug into Porter's shoulders as she fought to breathe around the two large cocks that had filled her to overflowing.

"Fuck, Hannah! Your ass is like a wet dream, all hot and tight. Are you okay, honey?" Edward asked.

"I'm good. I'd be better if someone would start moving. I need to move, guys!"

Porter shoved up as Edward pulled back, then they switched directions and he pulled back as Edward shoved forward. They stroked in and out of her welcoming body in long slow strokes, slowly increasing the tempo and power behind each thrust until finally, they were powering in and out of her amazing body.

The sound of their skin hitting paired with the moans and groans that escaped as they pushed higher and closer to climax seemed like music in the room to him. He wanted to hear Hannah scream in pleasure no matter if Edward helped get her there or not. All that mattered was that she was fulfilled and happy.

He reached under her pelvis to drag his finger across her exposed sex until he located the bundle of nerves that would help send her there faster. Faster at this point was better. He didn't know how Edward was fairing, but Porter was barely holding on by his toenails. His balls were tight against his body and burning with an unholy fire, the precursor to his fast approaching orgasm. He'd be damned if he came before she did.

"Aw, hell, Porter. I'm losing it."

"I've got her," he hissed out as he circled her clit then rubbed it with the tip of his finger.

Her sudden gasp was all the warning he had before her entire body bucked over him as she screamed out both of their names. He heard Edward curse behind her then all Porter knew was the blinding pleasure of Hannah's sweet body milking his cock as he climaxed so hard and so long he thought he would pass out.

His dick ached as his cum filled her hot cunt. The way she writhed around him added even more friction to the mess that was their lovemaking. He didn't even have the strength once he'd finished coming inside out to yell at Edward to move off of them. Instead, he bent one knee and used his foot as leverage to turn all three of them to the side with a long groan. Hannah didn't say one word or issue a single noise.

He peeled his eyes open and focused on her face to find her eyes closed and a soft smile on her face. When he nudged her with one hand, she didn't say a word and her head lolled to one side. She was out for the count. They'd fucked her to sleep. He wasn't sure whether to be proud or insulted.

Instead, Porter chuckled softly. "Hey, Ed. She's sound assed asleep. Think we bored her?"

Edward made a huffing noise. "She's probably worn out from coming. I know I am. If you'd shut up, I'd be asleep, too."

Porter yawned and silently supported that idea. He could use a nap right about then. They could take a quick clean up shower in a couple of hours. He relaxed one arm across Hannah's back and forgot all about the other man lying right up next to him as he dozed off.

* * * *

Hannah sighed as she woke feeling scrunched up and sticky all over. Why was she sticky? Then it all came back to her and she felt her skin burn with the knowledge that they'd fallen asleep in a heap after mind-blowing sex.

No. We made love. I love them. I can't pretend that I don't. It feels too good.

Hannah couldn't believe how good they were to her. Not only did they make sure she had plenty to eat and drink, but they made sure she was well satisfied in bed as well. Even if this was only the honeymoon stage and they slacked off some later, she would never forget how good they'd treated her in the beginning, especially considering she'd tricked them.

Not going there again. I promised myself I would dwell on that. It's over, in the past.

When she slowly managed to extract herself from between the two men, she nearly blew it all by laughing out loud at the picture they made when she stood at the foot of the bed looking at them.

Porter was flat on his back with one arm stretched over his head and the other across his chest. Edward was on his side, facing Porter with one arm nestled between the two of them and the other one resting on the other man's shoulder. It looked almost as if he was whispering in Porter's ear. They were going to flip!

She tip toed into the bathroom and closed the door in hopes she wouldn't wake them. She'd forgotten to look at the clock, but considering the moons were still shining through the window, she figured it was still night. She was sure the guys needed the sleep since they were starting their days out in the fields.

Her body ached in a glorious way. She felt stretched and massaged all at the same time. As she turned on the shower, she suddenly wanted something to drink. She found herself starting to turn and head to the kitchen.

"What the…" She stopped and frowned. She could get something to drink after her shower. She wasn't really dying of thirst like she seemed to think she was.

Once the water was warm enough, Hannah stepped in and quickly soaped up then rinsed off, just planning to remove the stickiness of her men's seed along with her own sweat for now. She could take a proper shower in the morning when she got up.

By the time she'd gotten out of the shower and dried off, she was almost anxious with the need to get something to drink. She caught herself almost bending over the sink to get a mouth full of the water. What was going on? Had any of the other women who'd been pregnant had these urges? She'd have to call Lacy up on the radio after the men had left to ask her. She didn't want to worry the men if it was something natural to pregnancy on Alpha.

Hannah made herself slow down on the stairs so she wouldn't miss a step and fall. Then she forced herself to get a glass from the cabinet instead of drinking straight from the pitcher. She downed two full glasses of the stone berry lemonade before she felt quenched. She'd just rinsed out her glass when she heard the guy's voices as they walked down the stairs. She turned and waited by the sink for them to appear in the doorway.

Both of them wore jeans open at the waist and nothing else. They also had scowls on their faces the likes she'd never seen before. It was all she could do not to burst out laughing at their expressions.

"Don't you dare laugh, little girl. I ought to turn you over my knee and paddle that sweet behind," Porter said with a mock growl.

"What's wrong? You both look as if someone stole your favorite toy," she said rolling her lips inward to hide her smile.

"You left us sleeping together, that's what's wrong. You don't leave us in the bed together like that," Edward said in a snarling voice.

Hannah wasn't worried. She could see the dancing laughter in his sparkling eyes. He might not have been comfortable waking up that way, but he wasn't really mad at her. She decided to play it up some more.

"All I did was take a quick shower and come downstairs to get something to drink. I didn't do anything."

"Don't try and act all innocent with us, sweetness. We know you posed us after you got up. There's no way we would have been against each other like that otherwise. You were between us." Porter stuck his hands on his hips and glared.

"Actually, I was sort of on top of you, Porter, and Edward was on my back. When I got out from between the two of you, well, you just collapsed on each other and I left you that way. I didn't think you'd want to wake up so early." She batted her eyelashes at the two men then screeched as they lunged at her.

Hannah ran around the table laughing but they split up on her and sandwiched her between them in the end. She couldn't help but laugh as they struggled to figure out where to put their hands with her between them like that.

"Are you through down here? We need to get back to sleep. It's nearly two and Porter and I need to be up early." Edward faced her and gave her a quick kiss.

"I'm ready. I just needed something to drink." The two men stepped back from her so they could all head back upstairs.

"Oh, wait. Let's see if that animal is out there since it's still dark out." Hannah hurried over to the window and peered out into the moonlit night.

She felt both men behind her, the heat from their bare chests warming her back. She didn't see anything moving around at first and started to back away when movement close to the house caught her attention.

"There. Look. Do you can it?" she squealed pointing in that direction.

"What the hell?" Edward's face pressed against the glass as he tried to see where she was pointing.

Porter frowned then walked over to the back door. "Stay there. I want to see if it will run off when I open the door. Watch for me."

Hannah all but held her breath as Porter threw open the door and stepped out, looking in the general direction of where the creature had been. She saw it jerk at the sound of the door opening, but it didn't run off right away. Then Porter's body was in the way and she couldn't see anything.

"Where did it go?" she squealed as Edward grabbed her and pulled her behind him.

"It walked up closer to Porter. Now it's turned and is running off toward the fence line," Edward said.

"I'll be damned. Did you see that?" Porter closed the door after stepping back inside. "It started to come toward me then decided to leave instead."

"Did you get a good look at it?" Edward asked.

"It looks just like what Hannah drew. It looks bigger than what I expected and it has near perfect hands. Both sets are like little hands. They look like monkey's hands," Porter said shaking his head.

"We'll need to check the fence to see how it got in. I guess with paws like those it could climb easily enough. Did you see teeth?" Edward asked.

"No. I didn't see any teeth. It has a flat bill-like snout, like a platypus and a duck all rolled up together. It had really small eyes though and they were squinted up like the moon light was hurting them or something." Porter checked the door to be sure it was locked. "Can't wait to talk to the others about that. I wonder if anyone has seen one before."

"Let's get back to bed. It will be time to get up soon enough," Edward said with a yawn.

Hannah was excited that they'd seen what she'd found the night before. Until then, she'd felt as if it might have been a figment of her imagination. Now she felt vindicated even though the men had never acted as if they doubted her. How she was going to sleep, she had no idea. She was too revved up to just fall asleep. Oddly enough, that was exactly what she did almost as soon as her head hit the pillow.

She noticed that neither man climbed on the bed until she'd settled in the middle though. Had she not fallen asleep, she would have teased them. Instead, she'd have to remember to do it later. It was as if a switch had been thrown and her eyes closed as her body relaxed. Just like that, she was gone.

Chapter Fourteen

Edward and Porter stretched as they climbed out of the transport. Five had come early after getting up in the middle of the night. Hannah had insisted on getting up with them to fix their breakfast and pack their lunches. He couldn't say he was sorry either. She was a great cook and it had been nice to be able to hold and kiss her good-bye before they'd left.

Now as they waited for Cam and Phillip to drive up, Edward wondered what she would do all day. There hadn't been any weeds yet for her to deal with, but they had found a hole where the crafty creature had dug his way through. It worried them that he could come and go. There was no way to keep him out. All they could really do was keep a watch and fill in the holes.

"There they are." Porter pointed at the slowly materializing dot on the horizon that soon became a transport like theirs.

When the other two men jumped down to greet them, Edward was suddenly antsy to ask them about the stranger animal.

"Hey, we saw an odd-looking thing last night. Hannah had already seen it the night before but it looks like this." Edward handed them the picture she'd drawn.

Porter filled them in on his take on the creature and how it had reacted when he'd opened the door. Cam and Phillip nodded as they passed the drawing back to them.

"That's an animal we don't know much about at all. Actually, we've never gotten close enough to get a good look of one before. They were devastating our crops when we first got here, but now we don't see as much of them or their damage as we did to begin with," Phillip said. "Cam's got a theory but it's sort of farfetched."

"What sort of theory?" Edward asked. "Is it dangerous? I don't like leaving Hannah there alone when it can come and go all it wants to."

"We don't think it's dangerous. We've never seen teeth on it, but that doesn't mean anything," Cam said. "The thing is, it would root up our plants when we first started planting. It did a lot of damage. We staked it out, trying to get a good glimpse of what it was so we could figure out how to stop it. We only saw parts of it though. It would be coming up out of the ground then disappear again."

"We tried shooting at it, but the thing was fast and just buried itself underground too fast for us to catch it," Phillip interrupted.

"Then they didn't seem to be messing with our crops anymore and we thought maybe we'd scared it off and there weren't enough of them around to bother us with the small area we were cultivating," Cam continued.

"So it isn't a problem anymore?" Porter asked.

"No. Actually, if Cam's theory is correct, we need the little buggers," Phillip said with a chuckle.

"What do you mean?" Edward asked, frowning.

"Sometimes when you're out checking the crops and moving the irrigation systems around, you'll end up with your foot in a hole. It's one of theirs, so be careful so you don't break an ankle or a leg." Cam leaned back against their transport. "They aren't digging up the plants because they want them to grow. They eat some of the roots beneath the plants. I think that their digging beneath the ground helps aerate the roots in this rich soil, stirring up the nitrogen they need to grow faster. Also, we don't have bugs or insects here to pollinate the plants. It's the animals that help spread it so that we get our fruits and vegetables."

"I had wondered how that happens without insects to spread the pollen. I was picturing us out here trying to germinate plants all day," Porter said with a sigh.

"That's why most of the trees around here are so short. The larger animals are what help spread the pollen and again, the seeds. Those mantis things are the tallest creatures we've seen so far. Without something taller, there's no way the seeds would be created," Cam explained.

"So these creatures that burrow below ground are shaking the plants so that they pollinate each other," Edward said astounded.

"That's my theory anyway. So far, we don't know how else it's happening. We haven't seen special bugs come out at night so there isn't much else that would explain it," Cam said.

"The only other possibility," Phillip began, "is that the near constant mild wind helps the process. It's always windy to a certain degree here, so get used to it."

"This place is weird," Porter said, shaking his head.

Edward agreed with him there. Still, they had a better chance at survival here than they did back on Earth. He'd take his chances here. He just had to figure out how to keep Hannah safe. She meant everything to him. He loved her so…

Whoa! Love? I'm in love with her? I can't be this quick.

"What do you think, Edward?" Porter asked him.

"What? Sorry. I was thinking about that animal," he lied.

"We're going to work on moving the irrigation equipment through the fields today while they finish planting the last few fields they have on this side." Porter watched him with an odd expression on his face.

"Sounds good. How far apart are the wells we'll be using? Do we need extra water pipes?" he asked.

"Shouldn't today. The wells are pretty evenly placed so that we don't weaken the pipes by having to screw too many together," Phillip said. "Keeps us from having to monitor them so closely with so few of us. There aren't any leaks to drown a field that way."

Edward nodded and the four men broke up to attend to their assigned duties for the day. Edward continued to toss around the idea that he'd fallen in love with Hannah. It wasn't as if there was anything wrong with loving her. He was just worried it was too soon. He didn't want to inadvertently say something that she'd take as him being flippant about it when he was serious.

"How are you feeling about leaving Hannah alone now that we know she's pregnant?" Porter asked out of the blue nearly an hour later.

"I don't much like it, but we don't have a lot of choice," Edward admitted.

"Yeah, Phillip and Cam talked about it being hard when Lacy had been pregnant. Still, they said once she got closer to time one of us should stay with her." Porter pushed on the wheels of the irrigation line they were moving.

"How are we going to know when to start staying home with her? They said she wouldn't last more than six or seven months at the most. That's weird, too. Why not nine months like back on Earth? We're still originally from Earth." Edward didn't like thinking that they were already changing to something different.

"I've been wondering that myself. I thought about the fact that we have an extra hour in our day, so that would cut a little out of her pregnancy. Then there's the fact that we're eating food grown on this planet and have some sort of weird-assed cell or enzyme in our systems now that could have some affect on how long it lasts," Porter said.

"I sure hope we made the right decision to come here, Porter."

"What choice did we have? I mean besides the fact that Earth is a ticking time bomb about to go off, they didn't exactly give us much of a choice when they recruited us."

Edward nodded absently as he set the break on the irrigation boom. "I hadn't really thought about that at the time, but you're right. They didn't really ask, they just told us where to go and when to be there. I suppose we could have refused, but that would have been suicide."

"Some of the women weren't given a choice even when they said they wanted to stay with their families," Porter pointed out. "I don't know for certain, but I heard rumors that they actually took some women from their husbands because they were still fertile and their husbands didn't have any skills they thought would lend themselves to colonizing a new planet."

"I hadn't heard that. I don't know what I would have done if I'd been married and they wanted my wife but didn't want me. I mean, she'd have a chance at living, whereas, if she stayed behind, she'd die for sure. How do you make that kind of decision?" Edward felt as if someone had walked across his grave with the shiver that ran down his spine.

"I guess you don't have to worry about it since you wouldn't have been making a choice. They'd have just taken her from you," Porter reminded him.

"Hell. No more talk like this. It's depressing and we need to be upbeat and happy that we're here and alive. We've got a son on the way and a wonderful, amazing wife at home waiting on us," he said, shoving all the negative crap out of his head.

"You're right. We're lucky to have her. We could have been stuck with Gladys," Porter quipped.

"Bite your tongue." Edward grinned. He had a quick thought that he owed the other woman a thank-you for skipping out on them. Thank goodness he'd never have to tell her though.

"Okay. Last one for the morning. I'm ready for lunch. What about you?" Porter asked him.

"Sounds good to me." He followed the other man back toward where they had parked the buggy. "Have you seen any of the holes Phillip and Cam were talking about?"

"One. I nearly stepped in it when we pulled that first system over."

Edward frowned. Had he seen any? He couldn't remember now. He started paying attention and found that he saw several just between there and where the transport was parked. He seemed to naturally avoid them somehow. He shook his head at the oddness of it. How did he know where to avoid putting his foot? It wasn't like he normally paid that close attention to where he walked. Normally he was too busy manhandling the danged irrigation equipment to look down at his feet.

If he didn't step in a hole or nearly step in one by the end of the day, he'd talk to Porter about it then. It all just seemed silly now that he was sitting down and eating. He could clearly see several of the small holes scattered around where they were eating. How could you possibly manage not to step in one when you weren't paying attention? They seemed to be everywhere.

"Wonder what Hannah will have for dinner tonight?" Porter asked.

"Don't know, but I bet it'll be delicious. That woman can cook. She even makes homemade bread better than my grandmother used to. I'd hate to have to keep that a secret when I visited her on Sundays."

"No kidding. She mentioned something about making a pie out of some of the natural fruits on the planet. I wonder if she'll do that today for dessert tonight." Porter licked his lips with a look of anticipation in his eyes.

"You don't look like someone thinking about a fruit pie. You've got sex on your mind," Edward said with a grin.

"That's because you've got the same dirty thoughts. I can already taste her sweet juices," Porter said with a smile of his own.

"I still can't get over how hot and tight she feels no matter where I am inside of her," Edward said.

"I know. Makes it hard to decide how to love on her. I don't want to have to choose. I just want to have all of her," Porter admitted.

"You love her?" Edward asked before he could stop himself.

Porter's mouth fell open. Then he closed it and nodded. "Yeah. I love her. She makes me the happiest man alive."

Edward nodded then grinned. "I'm the other happy fool. I love her, too. I was just trying to figure out how to keep from blurting it out to her."

"Why?" Porter frowned at him. "You need to tell her."

"I don't hear you telling her," Edward snarled. "I'm afraid she'll think it's too soon and I'm just saying the words without meaning them."

Porter sobered. "That's why I haven't said anything either. I mean maybe there is such a thing as love at first sight, but telling her too soon might not make it seem as special to her."

"How are we going to know when it's the right time? If we wait until she tells us, she'll think we're just saying it because she did." Edward ran a hand over his face.

Falling in love was a lot harder than it looked. There were way too many decisions that were attached to it. Making the wrong one could screw everything up from the beginning.

"Let's just tell her when the mood strikes us. Don't try and keep it to yourself. If you feel like saying it, then say it. I would think she could tell that we mean it." Porter's words made sense, but Edward had always been more cautious than most people.

"I'll think about it."

"Don't think it to death, Edward, or you might screw up and miss out."

"I won't."

* * * *

Nothing had prepared her for how long the day was going to be without the men there with her. She missed them. Their presence filled every room the moment they walked in, and without them she felt more than a little lost. How was she supposed to get through an entire day without them? Day after long, boring day.

Hannah frowned. What was wrong with her? She'd never been whiney or needy before. She needed to call Lacy and ask the other woman about her weird behaviors. She'd gotten busy fixing the men their breakfast and lunch that morning and forgotten. This was a good time.

With that thought in mind, she grabbed another glass of the stone berry lemonade and carried it with her to the office. After messing with the chair so she'd be comfortable, Hannah fiddled with the dial on the base unit until she had it where she thought it was supposed to be. Then she pressed in on the mike and spoke up.

"Um, Lacy? Are you around? Out." She nearly forgot to say *out* every time. Seemed stupid to her.

She waited then repeated her greeting again, waiting a minute or two in between each call. Finally, just when she was about to give up, Lacy's voice greeted her.

"Hi, Hannah, it's Lacy, out."

"I got you! I actually had it in the right place. How are you doing? Um, out." Hannah wasn't sure how to talk on the stupid thing. Why couldn't they just use it like a cell phone?

Hannah heard a chuckle come across the speaker. "I'm fine. Julie has been keeping me busy today. She's down for a nap now, thank goodness. Out."

"Um, can we not say out after every sentence?" she asked without saying out.

"Fine with me. I never do when I talk to the others. I do when I talk to the guys though. They're sticklers for following directions." Lacy's soft chuckle let Hannah know she was smiling.

"I wanted to ask some questions if you have time," she said.

"Go right ahead. I'm just relaxing with some tea while Julie is sleeping."

"Well, I'm not really sure where to begin. Um when you were pregnant, did you get really thirsty and hungry out of the blue?" She stopped, waiting to see what Lacy would say.

"Well, we figured out that I needed to eat and drink a lot more. I usually ate about five or six small meals a day, but I didn't really start getting that way until maybe I was two weeks along. Are you that far along?" Lacy asked.

Hannah gasped. "No. I'm only a few days. That's why I'm asking. It's scaring me."

"Um, are you certain there's not a chance you could be farther along than you are?"

"Oh, I'm certain all right. No exposure means no possibility." She could feel her face heating. It was dumb for her to be embarrassed talking over the radio to another woman about sex and babies.

"They you must just be anticipating the hunger. I don't think you should be that hungry already."

"Well, I sort of thought that, too, but I swear it's like something is telling me I'm dying of thirst and I start heading for the kitchen before I even realize it."

"Besides the hunger and thirst, is there anything else?" Lacy asked.

"I got sick yesterday after waking up from a nap. I thought it would be too early to have morning sickness, too," she said.

"Now that I'm not so sure of. I remember getting sick really early, but I'm not sure how early it was. The good thing is that it passes fast, or at least it did for me and for most of the other women. Elissa lives closer to me than you do and she had the same issue of early morning sickness."

"Is there anything more I should be on the lookout for? The weird feeling of having someone telling me what to do is driving me crazy."

Lacy was quiet for so long that Hannah wondered if she'd lost contact with her. She cleared her throat and called out.

"Lacy? Are you still there?"

"Yeah. I'm here. This is going to sound odd, but do you think that maybe your son is trying to direct you to what he wants or needs?"

"But he's just a little seed right now, right? How could he be able to do that at only a few days old?"

"He's about four or five days old, right?"

"Um yeah, I suppose." Hannah was really getting an odd feeling about this.

"Well, that might be more like four or five weeks in Alpha time. I don't know, but it would be interesting to have an ultrasound and find out what Dr. Jeff thinks." Lacy's voice sounded almost excited.

Hannah didn't really feel that way right now herself. She was more worried about what to expect and how to deal with a kid that was already that advanced if what Lacy was suggesting was true. It scared the crap out of her.

"Hannah? Are you okay?" Lacy's voice was full of concern.

"I'm going to kill the guys for this," she muttered.

"Why?" Lacy asked with obvious amusement in her voice.

"It's their fault. They immediately started talking to him when we got home the other night. I'm sure he never would have started this if they weren't egging him on." Hannah felt like screaming.

Lacy's laughter sounded warm over the radio's speaker, but it didn't make her feel much better. She wasn't the one living with a mini-me inside of her telling her what to do.

"It sounds to me like you're just really attuned to what he needs and reacting to it. He's hungry so you get hungry. He's thirsty so you get thirsty," Lacy explained.

"But he gets all he needs all the time. My eating doesn't help him right then," she protested.

"Maybe he's attuned to you then and knows when your body is in need of something even when you aren't aware of it yet. Think of him as an early warning signal that you are getting low on fuel or water."

"Lacy. I'm not sure you're my friend right now."

The other woman's laughter flowed over the radio speakers once more. "Hannah. I promise I am. I don't want you worrying over this. Our children are so much more than what we would have dreamed. It takes some getting used to and a lot of adjustment, but Julie is the joy of my life."

"I know," she said in almost a whisper. "I'm scared though. It really does feel like I'm losing control at times. Do you think if I told him to stop it, he would?"

"I'm not sure he has that much control yet, Hannah. He's probably only reacting right now and not actively directing you to do things. Talk to him though. Maybe in a few weeks you'll be able to actually communicate with him. Wouldn't that be amazing!"

"It would be something, all right," Hannah murmured.

"If he can communicate with you on some level, he can tell you if something is wrong or if he's having trouble. He might even be able to tell you when you're going to go into labor."

While Lacy's enthusiasm was nice, it didn't help Hannah's feelings much. The more she listened to the other woman, the more she wished she hadn't radioed her after all. Being ignorant sounded like a real blessing right about then.

"Don't worry, Hannah. As soon as you can go back to the space station, have the men take you to see Dr. Jeff to get a sonogram. Then you'll know about how far along you are."

"Okay. I'll do that. Thanks for talking with me, Lacy."

"I'm not sure you really mean that right now, but I understand. I've had a lot longer to get used to strange things here. Just call me up if you need me," Lacy said. "Out."

Hannah set the microphone back on the desk and slumped back in her chair. Was Lacy right? Was her baby reacting to her needs and influencing her to make sure she was eating and drinking when she needed to? Was that why she felt like someone was taking her over?

She needed to talk to the guys about this as soon as they got home. The thought that they might think she was crazy crossed her mind, but she would just make them call and talk to Lacy if they acted like they were worried about her sanity. She looked down at her belly and frowned. She had a little rounded poof there, but it was normal for her. She'd never had a flat belly to begin with.

"Listen, you. No more making me do what you want. If you think I need something to drink or eat, suggest that I'm hungry or thirsty. Don't try and make me follow orders like you've been doing. It's spooky as crap. Um, forget that word. You don't need to remember that word."

She shook her head and sighed. This was crazy. Still, it wouldn't hurt to try reasoning with the little thing. She might as well get comfortable if she was going to have a long talk with her yet-to-be-born son. It was nearly four and the men would be home around six. Dinner was in the oven so all she had to do was heat it up once they were ready to eat. That meant she could relax on the couch and if she fell asleep, them coming in would wake her up.

Hannah refreshed her glass of juice and settled on the couch on her side with her head on a pillow and her bare feet curled back. She lay there silent for several long minutes before finally gathering her courage to start.

"Hey there, butterbean. You know your daddies are planning to call you piggy if you don't stop making me eat all the time. I want you to know my voice, but I would like it if you wouldn't try and force me to do things. It really scares me." She sighed and lay there silently waiting for something to let her know if he understood her.

Lacy had told her that he might not have that much cognitive thinking yet. He might just be reacting to a need and not really understand what he was doing. How could she reason with him if he wasn't able to reason yet? Hannah didn't think she could handle the feeling of being taken over all the time. Not only was it annoying, it scared her that she'd do something she really didn't want to do. Losing control was frightening.

"Look, butterbean. I'm going to try to hold it together for a little longer while you develop some more in there. Just as soon as you understand me, remember not to try and make me do stuff. Suggest it or ask me or something. Don't just push me to do it. It's rude and it scares me."

She didn't have a clue if she'd made any headway with the munchkin, but she was leaning more and more to calling him mini-me instead of butterbean. It seemed much more fitting considering the issues he was causing. Of course, she hadn't talked to his fathers yet. They might laugh at her and brush her off. If they did, no more sex for them. She frowned. That meant no sex for her either. She didn't much like that punishment at all.

She got a strong urge to take a nap and cursed under her breath at the little minion. No doubt he was working his magic again and her little straight talk hadn't helped one bit. He was either ignoring her or flexing his muscle so to speak. Either way, Hannah was done for. She sure as heck hoped the guys had an idea of how to deal with the little dictator. Not even born yet and already she was waiting until his dads got home to take him to task.

Chapter Fifteen

"Are you serious?" Porter asked.

Hannah could tell he didn't believe her. She glanced over at Edward to see a similar expression on his face. Neither one of them believed her. She had hoped they would at least give her a little credit. If she had to get them to call Lacy and talk to her, she was going to be very pissed.

"Look. I've been having these urges, more like insistent demands, to eat or drink something off and on for a couple of days now. I even fell asleep last night without tossing and turning like I normally do when I'm wide awake. I mean as soon as my head hit the pillow, I was out like a light," she said.

"We did have some pretty amazing sex, honey," Edward said with a knowing grin.

"Dammit! Listen to me. I'm not kidding. Something is going on with me and I think it's the baby. Your son is trying to control me." Hannah heard herself and had to admit that it sounded crazy.

She sighed. "Look, you can call up Lacy and talk to her. She and I discussed it this afternoon and it's the only thing we can come up with to how I'm feeling."

"Baby. He's too young to be controlling you like that. I mean he hasn't even been alive for more than about four days," Porter said.

"Don't you think I know that? It's freaking me out." She sighed and put down her fork. She wasn't hungry anymore.

"It'll be okay, honey. Just relax and don't worry so much about everything. I'm sure finding out how advanced the children seem to be here has you on edge. I mean having little Julie telling you that you were pregnant already and that it was going to be a boy was wild enough," Edward said around a mouth full of the beef brisket she'd cooked.

She sighed and decided to just pretend she agreed with them for now. She wasn't going to convince them when it wasn't their body being bosses around.

"Eat, baby girl. You need to keep up your strength," Porter said with a frown.

"I had a late snack. I'm not very hungry right now." She retrieved the pitcher of tea from the fridge and refilled their glasses.

Hannah sat down and watched as they ate. She hadn't really asked them about their day yet. She'd jumped on them as soon as they'd sat down to eat with her issues with being taken over by a butterbean. Now she felt guilty. She should have asked about how things went in the fields and what they found out about the creature they'd seen.

"Did you ask Cam and Phillip about that creature?"

"Yeah. They hadn't seen it as closely as we have but knew about it. Seems that they've had trouble with it uprooting their plants at first but now it doesn't do much damage at all. They think it might actually be helping with the pollination," Edward said.

"Did they have a name for it?" she asked.

"Not really. Until now they've assumed it was a mole like creature and called it that. Now that we have a better description of it, it probably needs a name," Porter said.

"I want to name it. I just can't decide between platypig or a platymole. With that yellow skin and duck-like bill, it should have a unique name."

"Um, platypig? I don't know, Hannah." Porter looked amused.

"I know, but it isn't any worse than a muskie. I can't even being to understand that name," she said with a frown.

Both men laughed. She would think about it a little harder. If she got up in the middle of the night again, she'd see if it had come back and watch it. A name would come to her. She was determined to be the one to name this one.

Before she even realized it, she'd reached out and stabbed a piece of meat from Porter's plate and taken a bite off of it. She nearly choked on the expression that crossed Edward's face.

"Did you see that?" Edward asked.

Porter only nodded his head. Hannah had a feeling they might believe her now. The baby had decided she needed to eat again and she'd been ignoring it since she was depressed about their reaction to her announcement. Mini-me didn't seem to care what her state of mind was. Dammit, she needed to eat.

"Hannah? Are you okay, baby?" Porter asked.

She sighed. "I told you. I'm sorry I grabbed food off of your plate. I honestly didn't even know I was doing it until I'd already put it in my mouth."

"I believe you, baby. Your face was totally blank when you grabbed the meat. I don't freaking believe it." Porter sat back in his chair.

"Does it hurt when that happens?" Edward asked.

"No. I just sort of space out for a second then find myself getting something to eat or drink or wake up from a nap. It's annoying as hell."

Porter stabbed a piece of meat and cut it up for her on her plate. She sighed and stabbed a piece with her fork. It looked like she didn't have a choice when it came to the necessities. The baby was going to get his way one way or another. She'd have to learn to pout a different way.

After all of the dishes had been seen to, Hannah started to curl up on the couch while the men talked, but Porter seemed to have a different idea. He picked her up and carried her over to his recliner where he sat down and positioned her across his lap. Edward walked over and pulled her T-shirt over her head before she could think to protest.

"What are you guys doing?" she asked with a laugh.

"Having a talk with our son. You just sit here and be quiet. This doesn't concern you right now," Porter said.

She covered her smile and leaned back, amused that they suddenly believed her now. Let her go all possessed on them and suddenly she was telling the truth.

"Okay, butterbean, we need to have a chat, son," Porter began. He laid a gentle kiss on her belly. "No more taking over your mom's body. That's not nice. You can't go around making people do what you want them to do. You have to let them make their own decisions."

Edward cleared his throat. "We understand that you are only trying to take care of her and yourself, but it isn't the right way. Just let her know some other way that she needs to eat or get something to drink. Can't you make her stomach growl or something?"

Porter made a face at Edward. "Her stomach already growls on its own, man."

"Have you got a better idea?" he asked.

"Guys?"

Hannah was barely keeping it together. She was on the verge of bursting out laughing, and she was sure that would not go over well with them.

"Son. Let's have this talk every evening after we get home from work. Ed and I will always be here for you. We don't want you to ever think we aren't available. Now be a good boy and back off on the creepy shit…"

"Porter! Language! He can obviously hear you. Do you want the first word out of his mouth when he's born to be 'shit'?"

Edward did lose it then. He started laughing until he ended up on his knees next to the chair. Porter frowned at him then turned his glare toward her when she started giggling as well.

"I'm sorry. It's just so surreal to be talking to a baby that isn't even a week along yet. I know he's probably three weeks according to when he'll be born, but this is crazy," she said with a chuckle.

"You're the one who started it, baby. Now deal with it." Porter kissed her belly again then settled his chin on top of her head. "I love you, baby girl."

She stilled in his arms. Had she really heard him say that? She was scared to believe it.

"He's not the only one, honey." Edward kneeled up and kissed her lightly on the lips. "I love you, too."

"I don't know what to say. I was so afraid you'd never care for me like I do you. Then I realized it was more than caring for you. I love you both so much. You make me so happy," she said with tears in her eyes.

"I'm sorry I was an ass in the beginning. I don't deserve someone as special as you, Hannah. If it takes me the rest of my life, I'm going to make it up to you," Edward told her.

It was all she could do to keep from launching herself into his arms. Instead she pulled him down to kiss him, opening her mouth to his and reveling at the taste of him. He settled her where Porter lifted her up. She had the best of both worlds all rolled up in an amazing package. How had she ever gotten so lucky as to end up with two men who turned her inside out like they did?

"Okay. Enough of that, guys. I'm right here, you know." Porter's amused voice trying to sound disgusted finally penetrated their embrace.

Hannah wrapped one arm around his neck and turning, buried her face there. She nipped him there then released him and smiled.

"I might have tricked you into being my men, but unless it's freely given, I never would have had your love unless you truly wanted me. Thank you both for giving me the chance to earn your love."

"Hannah, you had us wrapped around your finger almost from the beginning. Now it looks like someone has you wrapped around his little finger. I can't wait to see what the future holds with you and our very talented son," Edward said with a wink. "Let the fun begin."

THE END

WWW.MARLAMONROE.COM

ABOUT THE AUTHOR

Marla Monroe has been writing professionally for about eleven years now. Her first book with Siren was published in January of 2011. She loves to write and spends every spare minute either at the keyboard or reading. She writes everything from sizzling-hot contemporary cowboys and dangerously addictive shifters to science fiction ménages with the occasional badass biker thrown in for good measure.

Marla lives in the southern US and works full-time at a busy hospital. When not writing, she loves to travel, spend time with her cats, and read. She's always eager to try something new and especially enjoys the research for her books. She loves to hear from readers about what they are looking for next.

You can reach Marla at themarlamonroe@yahoo.com, or visit her website at www.marlamonroe.com

My blog: www.themarlamonroe.blogspot.com

Twitter: @MarlaMonroe.1

Facebook: www.facebook.com/marla.monroe.7

For all titles by Marla Monroe, please visit
www.bookstrand.com/marla-monroe

Siren Publishing, Inc.
www.SirenPublishing.com